Beatrice Spalding.

Oct 3RD/48

THE OLD BEAUTY
AND OTHERS

The Old Beauty and Others

BY

WILLA CATHER

1 9  4 8

NEW YORK

ALFRED A KNOPF

CONTENTS

THE OLD BEAUTY

THE OLD BEAUTY

I

One brilliant September morning in 1922 a slender, fair-skinned man with white moustaches, waxed and turned up at the ends, stepped hurriedly out of the Hôtel Splendide at Aix-les-Bains and stood uncertainly at the edge of the driveway. He stood there for some moments, holding, or rather clutching, his gloves in one hand, a light cane in the other. The pavement was wet, glassy with water. The boys were still sprinkling the walk farther down the hill, and the fuchsias and dahlias in the beds sparkled with water drops. The clear air had the freshness of early morning and the smell of autumn foliage.

Two closed litters, carried by porters, came out of a side door and went joggling down the hill toward the baths. The gentleman standing on the kerb followed these eagerly with his eyes, as if about to dash after them; indeed, his mind seemed to accompany them to the turn in the walk where they disappeared, then to come back to him where he stood and at once to dart off in still another direction.

The gentleman was Mr. Henry Seabury, aged fifty-five, American-born, educated in England, and lately returned from a long business career in China. His evident nervousness was due to a shock: an old acquaintance, who had been one of the brilliant figures in the world of the 1890's, had died a few hours ago in this hotel.

As he stood there he was thinking that he ought to send telegrams . . . but to whom? The lady had no immediate family, and the distinguished men of her time who had cherished the slightest attention from her were all dead. No, there was one (perhaps the most variously gifted of that group) who was still living: living in seclusion down on the Riviera, in a great white mansion set in miles of park and garden. A cloud had come over this man in the midst of a triumphant public life. His opponents had ruined his career by a whispering campaign. They had set going a rumour which would have killed any public man in England at that time. Mr. Seabury began composing his telegram to Lord H—. Lord H— would recognize that this death was more than the death of an individual. To him her name would recall a society whose manners, dress, conventions, loyalties, codes of honour, were different from anything existing in the world today.

And there were certainly old acquaintances like himself, men not of her intimate circle, scattered about over the world; in the States, in China, India. But how to reach them?

Three young men came up the hill to resolve his perplexity; three newspaper correspondents, English, French, American. The American spoke to his companions. "There's the man I've seen about with her so much. He's the one we want."

The three approached Mr. Seabury, and the American addressed him. "Mr. Seabury, I believe? Excuse my stopping you, but we have just learned through the British Consulate that the former Lady Longstreet died in this hotel last night. We are newspaper men, and must send dispatches to our papers." He paused to introduce his companions by their names and the names of their journals. "We thought you might be good enough to tell us something about Lady Longstreet, Madame de Couçy, as she was known here."

"Nothing but what all the world knows." This intrusion had steadied Mr. Seabury, brought his scattered faculties to a focus.

"But we must jog the world's memory a little. A great many things have happened since Lady Longstreet was known everywhere."

"Certainly. You have only to cable your papers that Madame de Couçy, formerly Lady Longstreet, died here last night. They have in their files more than I could tell you if I stood here all morning."

"But the circumstances of her death?"

"You can get that from the management. Her life was interesting, but she died like anyone else — just as you will, some day."

"Her old friends, everywhere, would of course like to learn something about her life here this summer. No one knew her except as Madame de Couçy, so no one observed her very closely. You were with her a great deal, and the simple story of her life here would be — "

"I understand, but it is quite impossible. Good morning, gentlemen." Mr. Seabury went to his room to write his telegram to Lord H—.

II

Two months ago Henry Seabury had come here almost directly from China. His hurried trip across America and his few weeks in London scarcely counted. He was hunting for something, some spot that was still more or less as it used to be. Here, at Aix-les-Bains, he found the place unchanged, — and in the hotels many people very like those who used to come there.

The first night after he had settled himself at the Splendide he became interested in two old English ladies who dined at a table not far from his own. They had been coming here for many years, he felt sure. They had the old manner. They were at ease and reserved. Their dress was conservative. They were neither painted nor plucked, their nails were neither red nor green. One was plump, distinctly plump, indeed, but as she entered the dining-room he had noticed that she was quick in her movements and light on her feet. She was radiantly cheerful and talkative. But it was the other lady who interested him. She had an air of distinction, that unmistakable thing, which told him she had been a personage. She was tall, had a fine figure and carriage, but either she was much older than her friend, or life had used her more harshly. Something about her eyes and brow teased his memory. Had he once known her, or did she merely recall a type of woman he used to know? No, he felt that he must have met her, at least, long ago, when she was not a stern, gaunt-cheeked old woman with a yellowing complexion. The hotel management informed him that the lady was Madame de Couçy. He had never known anyone of that name.

The next afternoon when he was sitting under the plane trees in the *Place*, he saw the two ladies coming down the hill; the tall one moving with a peculiar drifting ease, looking into the distance as if the unlevel walk beneath her would naturally accommodate itself to her footing. She kept a white fur well up about her cheeks, though the day was hot. The short one tripped along beside her. They crossed the Square, sat down under the trees, and had tea brought out from the confectioner's. Then the muffled lady let her fur fall back a little and glanced about her. He was careful not to stare, but once, when he suddenly lifted his eyes, she was looking directly at him. He thought he saw a spark of curiosity, perhaps recognition.

The two ladies had tea in the *Place* every afternoon unless it rained; when they did not come

The Old Beauty

Seabury felt disappointed. Sometimes the taller one would pause before she sat down and suggest going farther, to the Casino. Once he was near enough to hear the rosy one exclaiming: "Oh, no! It's much nicer here, really. You are always dissatisfied when we go to the Casino. There are more of the kind you hate there."

The older one with a shrug and a mournful smile sat down resignedly in front of the pastry shop. When she had finished her tea she drew her wrap up about her chin as if about to leave, but her companion began to coax: "Let us wait for the newspaper woman. It's almost time for her, and I do like to get the home papers."

The other reminded her that there would be plenty of papers at the hotel.

"Yes, yes, I know. But I like to get them from her. I'm sure she's glad of our pennies."

When they left their table they usually walked about the Square for a time, keeping to the less frequented end toward the Park. They bought roses at the flower booths, and cyclamen from an old country woman who tramped about with a

basketful of them. Then they went slowly up the
hill toward the hotel.

III

Seabury's first enlightenment about these solitary women came from a most unlikely source.

Going up to the summit of Mont Revard in
the little railway train one morning, he made
the acquaintance of an English family (father,
mother, and two grown daughters) whom he
liked very much. He spent the day on the mountain in their company, and after that he saw a
great deal of them. They were from Devonshire,
home-staying people, not tourists. (The daughters had never been on the Continent before.)
They had come over to visit the son's grave in
one of the war cemeteries in the north of France.
The father brought them down to Aix to cheer
them up a little. (He and his wife had come there
on their honeymoon, long ago.) As the Thompsons were stopping at a cramped, rather mean little hotel down in the town, they spent most of
the day out of doors. Usually the mother and one

of the daughters sat the whole morning in the *Place*, while the other girl went off tramping with the father. The mother knitted, and the girl read aloud to her. Whichever daughter it happened to be kept watchful eye on Mrs. Thompson. If her face grew too pensive, the girl would close the book and say:

"Now, Mother, do let us have some chocolate and croissants. The breakfast at that hotel is horrid, and I'm famished."

Mr. Seabury often joined them in the morning. He found it very pleasant to be near that kind of family feeling. They felt his friendliness, the mother especially, and were pleased to have him join them at their chocolate, or to go with him to afternoon concerts at the Grand-Cercle.

One afternoon when the mother and both daughters were having tea with him near the Roman Arch, the two English ladies from his hotel crossed the Square and sat down at a table not far away. He noticed that Mrs. Thompson glanced often in their direction. Seabury kept his guests a long while at tea, — the afternoon was hot, and he knew their hotel was stuffy. He was telling the girls something about China, when the two unknown English ladies left their table and got into a taxi. Mrs. Thompson turned to Seabury and said in a low, agitated voice:

"Do you know, I believe the tall one of those two was Lady Longstreet."

Mr. Seabury started. "Oh, no! Could it be possible?"

"I am afraid it is. Yes, she is greatly changed. It's very sad. Six years ago she stayed at a country place near us, in Devonshire, and I used often to see her out on her horse. She still rode then. I don't think I can be mistaken."

In a flash everything came back to Seabury. "You're right, I'm sure of it, Mrs. Thompson. The lady lives at my hotel, and I've been puzzling about her. I knew Lady Longstreet slightly many years ago. Now that you tell me, I can see it. But . . . as you say, she is greatly changed. At the hotel she is known as Madame de Couçy."

"Yes, she married during the war; a Frenchman. But it must have been after she had lost her beauty. I had never heard of the marriage until he was killed, — in '17, I think. Then some of the English papers mentioned that he was the husband of Gabrielle Longstreet. It's very sad when those beautiful ones have to grow old, isn't it? We never have too many of them, at best."

The younger daughter threw her arms about Mrs. Thompson. "Oh, Mother, I wish you hadn't told us! I'm afraid Mr. Seabury does, too. It's such a shock."

He protested. "Yes, it is a shock, certainly. But I'm grateful to Mrs. Thompson. I must be very stupid not to have seen it. I'm glad to know. The two ladies seem very much alone, and the older one looks ill. I might be of some service, if she remembers me. It's all very strange: but one might be useful, perhaps, Mrs. Thompson?"

"That's the way to look at it, Mr. Seabury." Mrs. Thompson spoke gently. "I think she does remember you. When you were talking to Dorothy, turned away from them, she glanced at you often. The lady with her is a friend, don't you think, not a paid companion?"

The Old Beauty

He said he was sure of it, and she gave him a warm, grateful glance as if he and she could understand how much that meant, then turned to her daughters: "Why, there is Father, come to look for us!" She made a little signal to the stout, flushed man who was tramping across the Square in climbing boots.

IV

Mr. Seabury did not go back to his hotel for dinner. He dined at a little place with tables in the garden, and returned late to the Splendide. He felt rather knocked up by what Mrs. Thompson had told him, — felt that in this world people have to pay an extortionate price for any exceptional gift whatever. Once in his own room, he lay for a long while in a chaise longue before an open window, watching the stars and the fireflies, recalling the whole romantic story, — all he had ever known of Lady Longstreet. And in this hotel, full of people, she was unknown — she!

Gabrielle Longstreet was a name known all over the globe, — even in China, when he went there twenty-seven years ago. Yet she was not an actress or an adventuress. She had come into the European world in a perfectly regular, if somewhat unusual, way.

Sir Wilfred Longstreet, a lover of yachting and adventure on the high seas, had been driven into Martinique by a tropical hurricane. Strolling about the harbour town, he saw a young girl coming out of a church with her mother; the girl was nineteen, the mother perhaps forty. They were the two most beautiful women he had ever seen. The hurricane passed and was forgotten, but Sir Wilfred Longstreet's yacht still lay in the harbour of Fort de France. He sought out the girl's father, an English colonial from Barbados, who was easily convinced. The mother not so easily: she was a person of character as well as severe beauty. Longstreet had sworn that he would never take his yacht out to sea unless he carried Gabrielle aboard her. The *Sea Nymph* might lie and rot there.

In time the mother was reassured by letters and documents from England. She wished to do well for her daughter, and what very brilliant opportunities were there in Martinique? As for the girl, she wanted to see the world; she had never been off the island. Longstreet made a settlement upon Madame the mother, and submitted to the two services, civil and religious. He took his bride directly back to England. He had not advised his friends of his marriage; he was a young man who kept his affairs to himself.

He kept his wife in the country for some months. When he opened his town house and took her to London, things went as he could not possibly have foreseen. In six weeks she was the fashion of the town; the object of admiration among his friends, and his father's friends. Gabrielle was not socially ambitious, made no effort to please. She was not witty or especially clever, — had no accomplishments beyond speaking French as naturally as English. She said nothing memorable in either language. She was beautiful, that was all. And she was fresh. She came into that society of old London like a quiet country dawn.

She showed no great zest for this life so different from anything she had ever known; a quiet wonderment rather, faintly tinged with pleasure. There was no glitter about her, no sparkle. She never dressed in the mode: refused to wear crinoline in a world that billowed and swelled with it. Into drawing-rooms full of ladies enriched by marvels of hairdressing (switches, ringlets, puffs, pompadours, waves starred with gems), she came with her brown hair parted in the middle and coiled in a small knot at the back of her head. Hairdressers protested, as one client after another adopted the 'mode Gabrielle.' (The knot at the nape of the neck! Charwomen had always worn it; it was as old as mops and pails.)

The English liked high colour, but Lady Longstreet had no red roses in her cheeks. Her skin had the soft glow of orient pearls, — the jewel to which she was most often compared. She was not spirited, she was not witty, but no one ever heard her say a stupid thing. She was often called cold. She seemed unawakened, as if she were still an island girl with reserved island good manners. No woman had been so much discussed and argued about for a long stretch of years. It was to the older men that she was (unconsciously, as it seemed) more gracious. She liked them to tell her about events and personages already in the past; things she had come too late to see.

Longstreet, her husband, was none too pleased by the flutter she caused. It was no great credit to him to have discovered a rare creature; since everyone else discovered her the moment they had a glimpse of her. Men much his superiors in rank and importance looked over his head at his wife, passed him with a nod on their way to her. He began to feel annoyance, and waited for this flurry to pass over. But pass it did not. With her second and third seasons in town her circle grew. Statesmen and officers twenty years Longstreet's senior seemed to find in Gabrielle an escape from long boredom. He was jealous without having the common pretexts for jealousy. He began to spend more and more time on his yacht in distant waters. He left his wife in his town house with his spinster cousin as chaperone. Gabrielle's mother

came on from Martinique for a season, and was
almost as much admired as her daughter. Sir Wilfred found that the Martiniquaises had considerably overshadowed him. He was no longer the
interesting 'original' he had once been. His un-
expected appearances and disappearances were
mere incidents in the house and the life which
his wife and his cousin had so well organized. He
bore this for six years and then, unexpectedly, demanded divorce. He established the statutory
grounds, she petitioning for the decree. He made
her a generous settlement.

This brought about a great change in Gabrielle
Longstreet's life. She remained in London, and
bought a small house near St. James's Park. Longstreet's old cousin, to his great annoyance, stayed
on with Gabrielle, — the only one of his family
who had not treated her like a poor relation. The
loyalty of this spinster, a woman of spirit, Scotch
on the father's side, did a good deal to ease Gabrielle's fall in the world. For fall it was, of course.
She had her circle, but it was smaller and more
intimate. Fewer women invited her now, fewer of

the women she used to know. She did not go
afield for those who affected art and advanced
ideas; they would gladly have championed her
cause. She replied to their overtures that she no
longer went into society. Her men friends never
flinched in their loyalty. Those unembarrassed
by wives, the bachelors and widowers, were more
assiduous than ever. At that dinner table where
Gabrielle and "the Honourable MacPhairson,"
as the old cousin was called, were sometimes
the only women, one met promising young men,
not yet settled in their careers, and much older men, so solidly and successfully settled that
their presence in a company established its
propriety.

Nobody could ever say exactly why Gabrielle's
house was so attractive. The men who had the
entrée there were not skilful at defining such a
thing as 'charm' in words: that was not at all
their line. And they would have been reluctant to
admit that a negligible thing like temperature
had anything to do with the pleasant relaxation
they enjoyed there. The chill of London houses

had been one of the cruellest trials the young Martiniquaise had to bear. When she took a house of her own, she (secretly, as if it were a disgraceful thing to do) had a hot-air furnace put in her cellar, and she kept coal fires burning in the grates at either end of the drawing-room. In colour, however, the rooms were not warm, but rather cool and spring-like. Always flowers, and not too many. There was something more flower-like than the flowers, — something in Gabrielle herself (now more herself than ever she had been as Lady Longstreet); the soft pleasure that came into her face when she put out her hand to greet a hero of perhaps seventy years, the look of admiration in her calm grey eyes. A century earlier her French grandmothers may have greeted the dignitaries of the Church with such a look, — deep feeling, without eagerness of any kind. To a badgered Minister, who came in out of committee meetings and dirty weather, the warm house, the charming companionship which had no request lurking behind it, must have been grateful. The lingering touch of a white hand on his black sleeve can do a great deal for an elderly man who has left a busy and fruitless day behind him and who is worn down by the unreasonable demands of his own party. Nothing said in that room got out into the world. Gabrielle never repeated one man to another, — and as for the Honourable MacPhairson, she never gave anything away, not even a good story!

In time there came about a succession of Great Protectors, and Gabrielle Longstreet was more talked about than in the days of her sensational debut. Whether any of them were ever her lovers, no one could say. They were all men much older than she, and only one of them was known for light behaviour with women. Young men were sometimes asked to her house, but they were made to feel it was by special kindness. Henry Seabury himself had been taken there by young Hardwick, when he was still an undergraduate. Seabury had not known her well, however, until she leased a house in New York and spent two winters there. A jealous woman, and a very clever one, had made things unpleasant for her in London, and Gabrielle had quitted England for a time.

Sitting alone that night, recalling all he had heard of Lady Longstreet, Seabury tried to remember her face just as it was in the days when he used to know her; the beautiful contour of the cheeks, the low, straight brow, the lovely line from the chin to the base of the throat. Perhaps it was her eyes he remembered best; no glint in them, no sparkle, no drive. When she was moved by admiration, they did not glow, but became more soft, more grave; a kind of twilight shadow deepened in them. That look, with her calm white shoulders, her unconsciousness of her body and whatever clothed it, gave her the air of having come from afar off.

And now it was all gone. There was something tense, a little defiant in the shoulders now. The hands that used to lie on her dress forgotten, as a bunch of white violets might lie there . . . Well, it was all gone.

Plain women, he reflected, when they grow old

are — simply plain women. Often they improve. But a beautiful woman may become a ruin. The more delicate her beauty, the more it owes to some exquisite harmony in modelling and line, the more completely it is destroyed. Gabrielle Longstreet's face was now unrecognizable. She gave it no assistance, certainly. She was the only woman in the dining-room who used no make-up. She met the winter barefaced. Cheap counterfeits meant nothing to a woman who had had the real thing for so long. She must have been close upon forty when he knew her in New York, — and where was there such a creature in the world today? Certainly in his hurried trip across America and England he had not been gladdened by the sight of one. He had seen only cinema stars, and women curled and plucked and painted to look like them. Perhaps the few very beautiful women he remembered in the past had been illusions, had benefited by a romantic tradition which played upon them like a kindly light . . . and by an attitude in men which no longer existed.

v

When Mr. Seabury awoke the next day it was
clear to him that any approach to Madame de
Couçy must be made through the amiable-seem-
ing friend, Madame Allison as she was called at
the hotel, who always accompanied her. He had
noticed that this lady usually went down into the
town alone in the morning. After breakfasting he
walked down the hill and loitered about the little
streets. Presently he saw Madame Allison come
out of the English bank, with several small par-
cels tucked under her arm. He stepped beside her.

"Pardon me, Madame, but I am stopping at
your hotel, and I have noticed that you are a
friend of Madame de Couçy, whom I think I
used to know as Gabrielle Longstreet. It was
many years ago, and naturally she does not recognize me. Would it displease her if I sent up my
name, do you think?"

Mrs. Allison answered brightly. "Oh, she did
recognize you, if you are Mr. Seabury. Shall we
sit down in the shade for a moment? I find it very
warm here, even for August."

The Old Beauty

When they were seated under the plane trees she turned to him with a friendly smile and frank curiosity. "She is here for a complete rest and isn't seeing people, but I think she would be glad to see an old friend. She remembers you very well. At first she was not sure about your name, but I asked the porter. She recalled it at once and said she met you with Hardwick, General Hardwick, who was killed in the war. Yes, I'm sure she would be glad to see an old friend."

He explained that he was scarcely an old friend, merely one of many admirers; but he used to go to her house when she lived in New York.

"She said you did. She thought you did not recognize her. But we have all changed, haven't we?"

"And have you and I met before, Madame Allison?"

"Oh, drop the Madame, please! We both speak English, and I am Mrs. Allison. No, we never met. You may have seen me, if you went to the Alhambra. I was Cherry Beamish in those days."

"Then I last saw you in an Eton jacket, with your hair cropped. I never had the pleasure of seeing you out of your character parts, which accounts for my not recognizing — "

She cut him short with a jolly laugh. "Oh, thirty years and two stone would account, would account perfectly! I always did boy parts, you remember. They wouldn't have me in skirts. So I had to keep my weight down. Such a comfort not to fuss about it now. One has a right to a little of one's life, don't you think?"

He agreed. "But I saw you in America also. You had great success there."

She nodded. "Yes, three seasons, grand engagements. I laid by a pretty penny. I was married over there, and divorced over there, quite in the American style! He was a Scotch boy, stranded in Philadelphia. We parted with no hard feelings, but he was too expensive to keep." Seeing the hotel bus, Mrs. Allison hailed it. "I *shall* be glad if Gabrielle feels up to seeing you. She is frightfully dull here and not very well."

VI

The following evening, as Seabury went into
the dining-room and bowed to Mrs. Allison, she
beckoned him to Madame de Couçy's table. That
lady put out her jewelled hand and spoke
abruptly.

"Chetty tells me we are old acquaintances,
Mr. Seabury. Will you come up to us for coffee
after dinner? This is the number of our apartment." As she gave him her card he saw that her
hand trembled slightly. Her voice was much
deeper than it used to be, and cold. It had always
been cool, but soft, like a cool fragrance, — like
her eyes and her white arms.

When he rang at Madame de Couçy's suite an
hour later, her maid admitted him. The two ladies were seated before an open window, the coffee table near them and the percolator bubbling.
Mrs. Allison was the first to greet him. In a moment she retired, leaving him alone with Madame
de Couçy.

"It is very pleasant to meet you again, after so

many years, Seabury. How did you happen to come?"

Because he had liked the place long ago, he told her.

"And I, for the same reason. I live in Paris now. Mrs. Allison tells me you have been out in China all this while. And how are things there?"

"Not so good now, Lady Longstreet, may I still call you? China is rather falling to pieces."

"Just as here, eh? No, call me as I am known in this hotel, please. When we are alone, you may use my first name; that has survived time and change. As to change, we have got used to it. But you, coming back upon it, this Europe, suddenly . . . it must give you rather a shock."

It was she herself who had given him the greatest shock of all, and in one quick, penetrating glance she seemed to read that fact. She shrugged: there was nothing to be done about it. "Chetty, where are you?" she called.

Mrs. Allison came quickly from another room and poured the coffee. Her presence warmed the atmosphere considerably. She seemed unperturbed by the grimness of her friend's manner; and she herself was a most comfortable little person. Even her too evident plumpness was comfortable, since she didn't seem to mind it. She didn't like living in Paris very well, she said; something rather stiff and chilly about it. But she often ran away and went home to see her nieces and nephews, and they were a jolly lot. Yes, she found it very pleasant here at Aix. And now that an old friend of Gabrielle's had obligingly turned up, they would have someone to talk to, and that would be a blessing.

Madame de Couçy gave a low, mirthless laugh. "She seems to take a good deal for granted, doesn't she?"

"Not where I am concerned, if you mean that. I should be deeply grateful for someone to talk to. Between the three of us we may find a great deal."

"Be sure we shall," said Mrs. Allison. "We have the past, and the present — which is really very interesting, if only you will let yourself think so. Some of the people here are very novel and amusing, and others are quite like people we used to know. Don't you find it so, Mr. Seabury?"

He agreed with her and turned to Madame de Couçy. "May I smoke?"

"What a question to ask in these days! Yes, you and Chetty may smoke. I will take a liqueur."

Mrs. Allison rose. "Gabrielle has a cognac so old and precious that we keep it locked in a cabinet behind the piano." In opening the cabinet she overturned a framed photograph which fell to the floor. "There goes the General again! No, he didn't break, dear. We carry so many photographs about with us, Mr. Seabury."

Madame de Couçy turned to Seabury. "Do you recognize some of my old friends? There are some of yours, too, perhaps. I think I was never sentimental when I was young, but now I travel with my photographs. My friends mean more to me now than when they were alive. I was too ignorant then to realize what remarkable men they were. I supposed the world was always full of great men."

She left her chair and walked with him about

the salon and the long entrance hall, stopping before one and another; uniforms, military and naval, caps and gowns; photographs, drawings, engravings. As she spoke of them the character of her voice changed altogether, — became, indeed, the voice Seabury remembered. The hard, dry tone was a form of disguise, he conjectured; a protection behind which she addressed people from whom she expected neither recognition nor consideration.

"What an astonishing lot they are, seeing them together like this," he exclaimed with feeling. "How can a world manage to get on without them?"

"It hasn't managed very well, has it? You may remember that I was a rather ungrateful young woman. I took what came. A great man's time, his consideration, his affection, were mine in the natural course of things, I supposed. But it's not so now. I bow down to them in admiration . . . gratitude. They are dearer to me than when they were my living friends, — because I understand them better."

Seabury remarked that the men whose pictures looked down at them were too wise to expect youth and deep discernment in the same person.

"I'm not speaking of discernment; that I had, in a way. I mean ignorance. I simply didn't know all that lay behind them. I am better informed now. I read everything they wrote, and everything that has been written about them. That is my chief pleasure."

Seabury smiled indulgently and shook his head. "It wasn't for what you knew about them that they loved you."

She put her hand quickly on his arm. "Ah, you said that before you had time to think! You believe, then, that I did mean something to them?" For the first time she fixed on him the low, level, wondering look that he remembered of old: the woman he used to know seemed breathing beside him. When she turned away from him suddenly, he knew it was to hide the tears in her eyes. He had seen her cry once, a long time ago. He had not forgotten.

He took up a photograph and talked, to bridge

over a silence in which she could not trust her voice. "What a fine likeness of X—! He was my hero, among the whole group. Perhaps his contradictions fascinated me. I could never see how one side of him managed to live with the other. Yet I know that both sides were perfectly genuine. He was a mystery. And his end was mysterious. No one will ever know where or how. A secret departure on a critical mission, and never an arrival anywhere. It was like him."

Madame de Couçy turned, with a glow in her eyes such as he had never seen there in her youth. "The evening his disappearance was announced . . . Shall I ever forget it! I was in London. The newsboys were crying it in the street. I did not go to bed that night. I sat up in the drawing-room until daylight; hoping, saying the old prayers I used to say with my mother. It was all one could do. . . . Young Harney was with him, you remember. I have always been glad of that. Whatever fate was in store for his chief, Harney would have chosen to share it."

Seabury stayed much longer with Madame de

Couçy than he had intended. The ice once broken, he felt he might never find her so much herself again. They sat talking about people who were no longer in this world. She knew much more about them than he. Knew so much that her talk brought back not only the men, but their period; its security, the solid exterior, the exotic contradictions behind the screen; the deep, claret-coloured closing years of Victoria's reign. Nobody ever recognizes a period until it has gone by, he reflected: until it lies behind one it is merely everyday life.

VII

The next evening the Thompsons, all four of them, were to dine with Mr. Seabury at the Maison des Fleurs. Their holiday was over, and they would be leaving on the following afternoon. They would stop once more at that spot in the north, to place fresh wreaths, before they took the Channel boat.

When Seabury and his guests were seated and the dinner had been ordered, he was aware that the mother was looking at him rather wistfully. He felt he owed her some confidence, since it was she, really, who had enlightened him. He told her that he had called upon Gabrielle Longstreet last evening.

"And how is she, dear Mr. Seabury? Is she less — less forbidding than when we see her in the Square?"

"She was on her guard at first, but that soon passed. I stayed later than I should have done, but I had a delightful evening. I gather that she is a little antagonistic to the present order, — indifferent, at least. But when she talks about her old friends she is quite herself."

Mrs. Thompson listened eagerly. She hesitated and then asked: "Does she find life pleasant at all, do you think?"

Seabury told her how the lady was surrounded by the photographs and memoirs of her old friends; how she never travelled without them. It had struck him that she was living her life over again, — more understandingly than she lived it the first time.

Mrs. Thompson breathed a little sigh. "Then I know that all is well with her. You have done so much to make our stay here pleasant, Mr. Seabury, but your telling us this is the best of all. Even Father will be interested to know that."

The stout man, who wore an ancient tail coat made for him when he was much thinner, came out indignantly. "Even Father! I like that! One of the great beauties of our time, and very popular before the divorce."

His daughter laughed and patted his sleeve. Seabury went on to tell Mrs. Thompson that she had been quite right in surmising the companion to be a friend, not a paid attendant. "And a very charming person, too. She was one of your cleverest music-hall stars. Cherry Beamish."

Here Father dropped his spoon into his soup. "What's that? Cherry Beamish? But we haven't had such another since! Remember her in that coster song, Mother? It went round the world, that did. We were all crazy about her, the boys called her Cherish Beamy. No monkeyshines for her, never got herself mixed up in anything shady."

"Such a womanly woman in private life," Mrs. Thompson murmured. "My Dorothy went to school with two of her nieces. An excellent school, and quite dear. Their Aunt Chetty does everything for them. And now she is with Lady Longstreet! One wouldn't have supposed they'd ever meet, those two. But then things *are* strange now."

There was no lull in conversation at that dinner. After the father had enjoyed several glasses of champagne he delighted his daughters with an account of how Cherry Beamish used to do the tipsy schoolboy coming in at four in the morning and meeting his tutor in the garden.

VIII

Mr. Seabury sat waiting before the hotel in a comfortable car which he now hired by the week. Gabrielle and Chetty drove out with him every day. This afternoon they were to go to Annecy by the wild road along the Echelles. Presently Mrs. Allison came down alone. Gabrielle was staying in bed, she said. Last night Seabury had dined with them in their apartment, and Gabrielle had talked too much, she was afraid. "She didn't sleep afterward, but I think she will make it up today if she is quite alone."

Seabury handed her into the car. In a few minutes they were running past the lake of Bourget.

"This gives me an opportunity, Mrs. Allison, to ask you how it came about that you've become Lady Longstreet's protector. It's a beautiful friendship."

She laughed. "And an amazing one? But I think you must call me Chetty, as she does, if we are to be confidential. Yes, I suppose it must seem to you the queerest partnership that war and desolation have made. But you see, she was so strangely left. When I first began to look after her a little, two years ago, she was ill in an hotel in Paris (we have taken a flat since), and there was no one, positively no one but the hotel people, the French doctor, and an English nurse who had chanced to be within call. It was the nurse, really, who gave me my cue. I had sent flowers, with no name, of course. (What would a bygone music-hall name mean to Gabrielle Longstreet?) And I called often to inquire. One morning I met Nurse Ames just as she was going out into the Champs-Élysées for her exercise, and she asked me to accompany her. She was an experienced woman, not young. She remembered when Gabrielle Longstreet's name and photographs were known all over the Continent, and when people at home were keen enough upon meeting her. And here she was, dangerously ill in a foreign hotel, and there was no one, simply no one. To be sure, she was registered under the name of her second husband."

Seabury interrupted. "And who was he, this de Couçy? I have heard nothing about him."

"I know very little myself, I never met him. They had been friends a long while, I believe. He was killed in action — less than a year after they were married. His name was a disguise for her, even then. She came from Martinique, you remember, and she had no relatives in England. Longstreet's people had never liked her. So, you see, she was quite alone."

Seabury took her plump little hand. "And that was where you came in, Chetty?"

She gave his fingers a squeeze. "Thank you! That's nice. It was Nurse Ames who did it. The war made a lot of wise nurses. After Gabrielle was well enough to see people, there was no one for her to see! The same thing that had happened to her friends in England had happened over here. The old men had paid the debt of nature, and the young ones were killed or disabled or had lost touch with her. She once had many friends in Paris. Nurse Ames told me that an old French officer, blinded in the war, sometimes came to see her, guided by his little granddaughter. She said her patient had expressed curiosity about the English woman who had sent so many flowers. I wrote a note, asking whether I could be of any service, and signed my professional name. She might recognize it, she might not. We had been on a committee together during the war. She told the nurse to admit me, and that's how it began."

Seabury took her hand again. "Now I want you to be frank with me. Had she then, or has she now, money worries at all?"

Cherry Beamish chuckled. "Not she, you may believe! But I have had a few for her. On the whole, she's behaved very well. She sold her place in Devonshire to advantage, before the war. Her capital is in British bonds. She seems to you harassed?"

"Sometimes."

Mrs. Allison looked grave and was silent for a little. "Yes," with a sigh, "she gets very low at times. She suffers from strange regrets. She broods on the things she might have done for her friends and didn't, — thinks she was cold to them. Was she, in those days, so indifferent as she makes herself believe?"

Seabury reflected. "Not exactly indifferent. She wouldn't have been so attractive if she'd been that. She didn't take things very hard, perhaps.

She used to strike me as . . . well, we might call it unawakened."

"But wasn't she the most beautiful creature then! I used to see her at the races, and at charity bazaars, in my early professional days. After the war broke out and everybody was all mixed up, I was put on an entertainment committee with her. She wasn't quite the Lady Longstreet of my youth, but she still had that grand style. It was the illness in Paris that broke her. She's changed very fast ever since. You see she thought, once the war was over, the world would be just as it used to be. Of course it isn't."

By this time the car had reached Annecy, and they stopped for tea. The shore of the lake was crowded with young people taking their last dip for the day; sunbrowned backs and shoulders, naked arms and legs. As Mrs. Allison was having her tea on the terrace, she watched the bathers. Presently she twinkled a sly smile at her host. "Do you know, I'm rather glad we didn't bring Gabrielle! It puts her out terribly to see young people bathing naked. She makes comments that are indecent, really! If only she had a swarm of young nieces and nephews, as I have, she'd see things quite differently, and she'd be much happier. Legs were never wicked to us stage people, and now all the young things know they are not wicked."

IX

When Madame de Couçy went out with Seabury alone, he missed the companionship of Cherry Beamish. With Cherry the old beauty always softened a little; seemed amused by the other's interest in whatever the day produced: the countryside, the weather, the number of cakes she permitted herself for tea. The imagination which made this strange friendship possible was certainly on the side of Cherry Beamish. For her, he could see, there was something in it; to be the anchor, the refuge, indeed, of one so out of her natural orbit, — selected by her long ago as an object of special admiration.

One afternoon when he called, the maid, answering his ring, said that Madame would not go

out this afternoon, but hoped he would stay and
have tea with her in her salon. He told the lift
boy to dismiss the car and went in to Madame de
Couçy. She received him with unusual warmth.

"Chetty is out for the afternoon, with some
friends from home. Oh, she still has a great many!
She is much younger than I, in every sense. Today I particularly wanted to see you alone. It's
curious how the world runs away from one, slips
by without one's realizing it."

He reminded her that the circumstances had
been unusual. "We have lived through a storm
to which the French Revolution, which used to
be our standard of horrors, was merely a breeze.
A rather gentlemanly affair, as one looks back on
it. . . . As for me, I am grateful to be alive, sitting here with you in a comfortable hotel (I
might be in a prison full of rats), in a France
still undestroyed."

The old lady looked into his eyes with the
calm, level gaze so rare with her now. "Are you
grateful? I am not. I think one should go out
with one's time. I particularly wished to see you

alone this afternoon. I want to thank you for your tact and gentleness with me one hideous evening long ago; in my house in New York. You were a darling boy to me that night. If you hadn't come along, I don't know how I would have got over it — out of it, even. One can't call the servants."

"But, Gabrielle, why recall a disagreeable incident when you have so many agreeable ones to remember?"

She seemed not to hear him, but went on, speaking deliberately, as if she were reflecting aloud. "It was strange, your coming in just when you did: that night it seemed to me like a miracle. Afterward, I remembered you had been expected at eight. But I had forgotten all that, forgotten everything. Never before or since have I been so frightened. It was something worse than fear."

There was a knock at the door. Madame de Couçy called: *"Entrez!"* without turning round. While the tea was brought she sat looking out of the window, frowning. When the waiter had gone she turned abruptly to Seabury:

"After that night I never saw you again until you walked into the dining-room of this hotel a few weeks ago. I had gone into the country somewhere, hiding with friends, and when I came back to New York, you were already on your way to China. I never had a chance to explain."

"There was certainly no need for that."

"Not for you, perhaps. But for me. You may have thought such scenes were frequent in my life. Hear me out, please," as he protested. "That man had come to my house at seven o'clock that evening and sent up a message begging me to see him about some business matters. (I had been stupid enough to let him make investments for me.) I finished dressing and hurried down to the drawing-room." Here she stopped and slowly drank a cup of tea. "Do you know, after you came in I did not see you at all, not for some time, I think. I was mired down in something . . . *the power of the dog,* the English Prayer Book calls it. But the moment I heard your voice, I knew that I was safe . . . I felt the leech drop off. I have never forgot the sound of your voice that night; so calm, with all a man's strength behind it, — and you were only a boy. You merely asked if you had come too early. I felt the leech drop off. After that I remember nothing. I didn't see you, with my eyes, until you gave me your handkerchief. You stayed with me and looked after me all evening.

"You see, I had let the beast come to my house, oh, a number of times! I had asked his advice and allowed him to make investments for me. I had done the same thing at home with men who knew about such matters; they were men like yourself and Hardwick. In a strange country one goes astray in one's reckonings. I had met that man again and again at the houses of my friends, — your friends! Of course his personality was repulsive to me. One knew at once that under his smoothness he was a vulgar person. I supposed that was not unusual in great bankers in the States."

"You simply chose the wrong banker, Gabrielle. The man's accent must have told you that he belonged to a country you did not admire."

"But I tell you I met him at the houses of decent people."

Seabury shook his head. "Yes, I am afraid you must blame us for that. Americans, even those whom you call the decent ones, do ask people to their houses who shouldn't be there. They are often asked *because* they are outrageous, — and therefore considered amusing. Besides, that fellow had a very clever way of pushing himself. If a man is generous in his contributions to good causes, and is useful on committees and commissions, he is asked to the houses of the people who have these good causes at heart."

"And perhaps I, too, was asked because I was considered notorious? A divorcée, known to have more friends among men than among women at home? I think I see what you mean. There are not many shades in your society. I left the States soon after you sailed for China. I gave up my New York house at a loss to be rid of it. The instant I recognized you in the dining-room downstairs, that miserable evening came back to me. In so far as our acquaintance was concerned, all that had happened only the night before."

"Then I am reaping a reward I didn't deserve, some thirty years afterward! If I had not happened to call that evening when you were so — so unpleasantly surprised, you would never have remembered me at all! We shouldn't be sitting together at this moment. Now may I ring for some fresh tea, dear? Let us be comfortable. This afternoon has brought us closer together. And this little spot in Savoie is a nice place to renew old friendships, don't you think?"

X

Some hours later, when Mr. Seabury was dressing for dinner, he was thinking of that strange evening in Gabrielle Longstreet's house on Fifty-third Street, New York.

He was then twenty-four years old. She had been very gracious to him all the winter.

On that particular evening he was to take her to dine at Delmonico's. Her cook and butler were excused to attend a wedding. The maid who answered his ring asked him to go up to the drawing-room on the second floor, where Madame was awaiting him. She followed him as far as the turn of the stairway, then, hearing another ring at the door, she excused herself.

He went on alone. As he approached the wide doorway leading into the drawing-room, he was conscious of something unusual; a sound, or perhaps an unnatural stillness. From the doorway he beheld something quite terrible. At the far end of the room Gabrielle Longstreet was seated on a little French sofa — not seated, but silently struggling. Behind the sofa stood a stout, dark man leaning over her. His left arm, about her waist, pinioned her against the flowered silk upholstery. His right hand was thrust deep into the low-cut bodice of her dinner gown. In her struggle she had turned a little on her side; her right arm was in the grip of his left hand, and she was trying to free the other, which was held down by the pressure of his elbow. Neither of those two made a sound. Her face was averted, half hidden

against the blue silk back of the sofa. Young Seabury stood still just long enough to see what the
situation really was. Then he stepped across the
threshold and said with such coolness as he could
command: "Am I too early, Madame Longstreet?"

The man behind her started from his crouch-
ing position, darted away from the sofa, and
disappeared down the stairway. To reach the
stairs he passed Seabury, without lifting his eyes,
but his face was glistening wet.

The lady lay without stirring, her face now
completely hidden. She looked so crushed and
helpless, he thought she must be hurt physically.
He spoke to her softly: "Madame Longstreet,
shall I call — "

"Oh, don't call! Don't call anyone." She began shuddering violently, her face still turned
away. "Some brandy, please. Downstairs, in the
dining-room."

He ran down the stairs, had to tell the solic-
itous maid that Madame wished to be alone for
the present. When he came back Gabrielle had

caught up the shoulder straps of her gown. Her right arm bore red finger marks. She was shivering and sobbing. He slipped his handkerchief into her hand, and she held it over her mouth. She took a little brandy. Then another fit of weeping came on. He begged her to come nearer to the fire. She put her hand on his arm, but seemed unable to rise. He lifted her from that seat of humiliation and took her, wavering between his supporting hands, to a low chair beside the coal grate. She sank into it, and he put a cushion under her feet. He persuaded her to drink the rest of the brandy. She stopped crying and leaned back, her eyes closed, her hands lying nerveless on the arms of the chair. Seabury thought he had never seen her when she was more beautiful . . . probably that was because she was helpless and he was young.

"Perhaps you would like me to go now?" he asked her.

She opened her eyes. "Oh, no! Don't leave me, please. I am so much safer with you here." She put her hand, still cold, on his for a moment, then closed her eyes and went back into that languor of exhaustion.

Perhaps half an hour went by. She did not stir, but he knew she was not asleep: an occasional trembling of the eyelids, tears stealing out from under her black lashes and glistening unregarded on her cheeks; like pearls he thought they were, transparent shimmers on velvet cheeks gone very white.

When suddenly she sat up, she spoke in her natural voice.

"But, my dear boy, you have gone dinnerless all this while! Won't you stay with me and have just a bit of something up here? Do ring for Hopkins, please."

The young man caught at the suggestion. If once he could get her mind on the duties of caring for a guest, that might lead to something. He must try to be very hungry.

The kitchen maid was in and, under Hopkins's direction, got together a creditable supper and brought it up to the drawing-room. Gabrielle took nothing but the hot soup and a little sherry.

Young Seabury, once he tasted food, found he had no difficulty in doing away with cold pheasant and salad.

Gabrielle had quite recovered her self-control. She talked very little, but that was not unusual with her. He told her about Hardwick's approaching marriage. For him, the evening went by very pleasantly. He felt with her a closer intimacy than ever before.

When at midnight he rose to take his leave, she detained him beside her chair, holding his hand. "At some other time I shall explain what you saw here tonight. How could such a thing happen in one's own house, in an English-speaking city . . . ?"

"But that was not an English-speaking man who went out from here. He is an immigrant who has made a lot of money. He does not belong."

"Yes, that is true. I wish you weren't going out to China. Not for long, I hope. It's a bad thing to be away from one's own people." Her voice broke, and tears came again. He kissed her hand softly, devotedly, and went downstairs.

He had not seen her again until his arrival at this hotel some weeks ago, when he did not recognize her.

XI

One evening when Mrs. Allison and Madame de Couçy had been dining with Seabury at the Maison des Fleurs, they went into the tea room to have their coffee and watch the dancing. It was now September, and almost everyone would be leaving next week. The floor was full of young people, English, American, French, moving monotonously to monotonous rhythms, — some of them scarcely moving at all. Gabrielle watched them through her lorgnette, with a look of resigned boredom.

Mrs. Allison frowned at her playfully. "Of course it's all very different," she observed, "but then, so is everything." She turned to Seabury: "You know we used to have to put so much drive into a dance act, or it didn't go at all. Lottie Collins was the only lazy dancer who could get anything over. But the truth was, the dear thing couldn't dance at all; got on by swinging her foot! There must be something in all this new manner, if only one could get it. That couple down by the bar now, the girl with the *very* low back: they are doing it beautifully; she dips and rises like a bird in the air . . . a tired bird, though. That's the disconcerting thing. It all seems so tired."

Seabury agreed with her cheerfully that it was charming, though tired. He felt a gathering chill in the lady on his right. Presently she said impatiently: "Haven't you had enough of this, Chetty?"

Mrs. Allison sighed. "You never see anything in it, do you, dear?"

"I see wriggling. They look to me like lizards dancing — or reptiles coupling."

"Oh, no, dear! No! They are such sweet young things. But they are dancing in a dream. I want to go and wake them up. They are missing so much fun. Dancing ought to be open and free, with the lungs full; not mysterious and breathless. I wish I could see a *spirited* waltz again."

Gabrielle shrugged and gave a dry laugh. "I

wish I could dance one! I think I should try, if by any chance I should ever hear a waltz played again."

Seabury rose from his chair. "May I take you up on that? Will you?"

She seemed amused and incredulous, but nodded.

"Excuse me for a moment." He strolled toward the orchestra. When the tango was over he spoke to the conductor, handing him something from his vest pocket. The conductor smiled and bowed, then spoke to his men, who smiled in turn. The saxophone put down his instrument and grinned. The strings sat up in their chairs, pulled themselves up, as it were, tuned for a moment, and sat at attention. At the lift of the leader's hand they began the "Blue Danube."

Gabrielle took Mr. Seabury's arm. They passed a dozen couples who were making a sleepy effort and swung into the open square where the line of tables stopped. Seabury had never danced with Gabrielle Longstreet, and he was astonished. She had attack and style, the grand style, slightly mil-

itary, quite right for her tall, straight figure. He
held her hand very high, accordingly. The conductor caught the idea; smartened the tempo
slightly, made the accents sharper. One by one
the young couples dropped out and sat down to
smoke. The two old waltzers were left alone on
the floor. There was a stir of curiosity about the
room; who were those two, and why were they
doing it? Cherry Beamish heard remarks from
the adjoining tables.

"She's rather stunning, the old dear!"

"Aren't they funny?"

"It's so quaint and theatrical. Quite effective
in its way."

Seabury had not danced for some time. He
thought the musicians drew the middle part out
interminably; rather suspected they were playing
a joke on him. But his partner lost none of her
brilliance and verve. He tried to live up to her.
He was grateful when those fiddlers snapped out
the last phrase. As he took Gabrielle to her seat,
a little breeze of applause broke out from the girls
about the room.

"Dear young things!" murmured Chetty, who was flushed with pleasure and excitement. A group of older men who had come in from the dining-room were applauding.

"Let us go now, Seabury. I am afraid we have been making rather an exhibition," murmured Madame de Couçy. As they got into the car awaiting them outside, she laughed good-humouredly: "Do you know, Chetty, I quite enjoyed it!"

XII

The next morning Mrs. Allison telephoned Seabury that Gabrielle had slept well after an amusing evening: felt so fit that she thought they might seize upon this glorious morning for a drive to the Grande-Chartreuse. The drive, by the route they preferred, was a long one, and hitherto she had not felt quite equal to it. Accordingly, the three left the hotel at eleven o'clock with Seabury's trusty young Savoyard driver, and were soon in the mountains.

It was one of those high-heavenly days that of-

ten come among the mountains of Savoie in autumn. In the valleys the hillsides were pink with
autumn crocuses thrusting up out of the short
sunburned grass. The beech trees still held their
satiny green. As the road wound higher and
higher toward the heights, Seabury and his companions grew more and more silent. The light-
ness and purity of the air gave one a sense of de-
tachment from everything one had left behind
"down there, back yonder." Mere breathing was
a delicate physical pleasure. One had the feeling
that life would go on thus forever in high places,
among naked peaks cut sharp against a stainless
sky.

Ever afterward Seabury remembered that drive
as strangely impersonal. He and the two ladies
were each lost in a companionship much closer
than any they could share with one another. The
clean-cut mountain boy who drove them seemed
lost in thoughts of his own. His eyes were on the
road: he never spoke. Once, when the gold tones
of an alpine horn floated down from some hidden
pasture far overhead, he stopped the car of his

own accord and shut off the engine. He threw a smiling glance back at Seabury and then sat still, while the simple, melancholy song floated down through the blue air. When it ceased, he waited a little, looking up. As the horn did not sing again, he drove on without comment.

At last, beyond a sharp turn in the road, the monastery came into view; acres of slate roof, of many heights and pitches, turrets and steep slopes. The terrifying white mountain crags overhung it from behind, and the green beech wood lay all about its walls. The sunlight blazing down upon that mothering roof showed ruined patches: the Government could not afford to keep such a wilderness of leading in repair.

The monastery, superb and solitary among the lonely mountains, was after all a destination: brought Seabury's party down into man's world again, though it was the world of the past. They began to chatter foolishly, after hours of silent reflection. Mrs. Allison wished to see the kitchen of the Carthusians, and the chapel, but she thought Gabrielle should stay in the car. Madame de

Couçy insisted that she was not tired: she would walk about the stone courtyard while the other two went into the monastery.

Except for a one-armed guard in uniform, the great court was empty. Herbs and little creeping plants grew between the cobblestones. The three walked toward the great open well and leaned against the stone wall that encircled it, looking down into its wide mouth. The hewn blocks of the coping were moss-grown, and there was water at the bottom. Madame de Couçy slipped a little mirror from her handbag and threw a sunbeam down into the stone-lined well. That yellow ray seemed to waken the black water at the bottom: little ripples stirred over the surface. She said nothing, but she smiled as she threw the gold plaque over the water and the wet moss of the lower coping. Chetty and Seabury left her there. When he glanced back, just before they disappeared into the labyrinth of buildings, she was still looking down into the well and playing with her little reflector, a faintly contemptuous smile on her lips.

The Old Beauty

After nearly two hours at the monastery the party started homeward. Seabury told the driver to regulate his speed so that they would see the last light on the mountains before they reached the hotel.

The return trip was ill-starred: they narrowly escaped a serious accident. As they rounded one of those sharp curves, with a steep wall on their right and an open gulf on the left, the chauffeur was confronted by a small car with two women, crossing the road just in front of him. To avoid throwing them over the precipice he ran sharply to the right, grazing the rock wall until he could bring his car to a stop. His passengers were thrown violently forward over the driver's seat. The light car had been on the wrong side of the road, and had attempted to cross on hearing the Savoyard's horn. His nerve and quickness had brought every one off alive, at least.

Immediately the two women from the other car sprang out and ran up to Seabury with shrill protestations; they were very careful drivers, had run this car twelve thousand miles and never had an accident, etc. They were Americans; bobbed, hatless, clad in dirty white knickers and sweaters. They addressed each other as "Marge" and "Jim." Seabury's forehead was bleeding: they repeatedly offered to plaster it up for him.

The Savoyard was in the road, working with his mudguard and his front wheel. Madame de Couçy was lying back in her seat, pale, her eyes closed, something very wrong with her breathing. Mrs. Allison was fanning her with Seabury's hat. The two girls who had caused all the trouble had lit cigarettes and were swaggering about with their hands in their trousers pockets, giving advice to the driver about his wheel. The Savoyard never lifted his eyes. He had not spoken since he ran his car into the wall. The sharp voices, knowingly ordering him to *"regardez, attendez,"* did not pierce his silence or his contempt. Seabury paid no attention to them because he was alarmed about Madame de Couçy, who looked desperately ill. She ought to lie down, he felt sure, but there was no place to put her — the road was cut along the face of a cliff for a long way back. Chetty had aromatic ammonia in her handbag; she persuaded Gabrielle to take it from the bottle, as they had no cup. While Seabury was leaning over her she opened her eyes and said distinctly:

"I think I am not hurt . . . faintness, a little palpitation. If you could get those creatures away . . ."

He sprang off the running-board and drew the two intruders aside. He addressed them; first politely, then forcibly. Their reply was impertinent, but they got into their dirty little car and went. The Savoyard was left in peace; the situation was simplified. Three elderly people had been badly shaken up and bruised, but the brief submersion in frightfulness was over. At last the driver said he could get his car home safely.

During the rest of the drive Madame de Couçy seemed quite restored. Her colour was not good, but her self-control was admirable.

"You must let me give that boy something on my own account, Seabury. Oh, I know you will be generous with him! But I feel a personal interest. He took a risk, and he took the right one. He couldn't run the chance of knocking two women over a precipice. They happened to be worth nobody's consideration, but that doesn't alter the code."

"Such an afternoon to put you through!" Seabury groaned.

"It was natural, wasn't it, after such a morning? After one has been *exaltée*, there usually comes a shock. Oh, I don't mean the bruises we got! I mean the white breeches." Gabrielle laughed, her good laugh, with no malice in it. She put her hand on his shoulder. "How ever did you manage to dispose of them so quickly?"

When the car stopped before the hotel, Madame de Couçy put a tiny card case into the driver's hand with a smile and a word. But when she tried to rise from the seat, she sank back. Seabury and the Savoyard lifted her out, carried her into the hotel and up the lift, into her own chamber. As they placed her on the bed, Seabury said he would call a doctor. Madame de Couçy opened her eyes and spoke firmly:

"That is not necessary. Chetty knows what to

do for me. I shall be myself tomorrow. Thank you both, thank you."

Outside the chamber door Seabury asked Mrs. Allison whether he should telephone for Doctor Françon.

"I think not. A new person would only disturb her. I have all the remedies her own doctor gave me for these attacks. Quiet is the most important thing, really."

The next morning Seabury was awakened very early, something before six o'clock, by the buzz of his telephone. Mrs. Allison spoke, asking in a low voice if he would come to their apartment as soon as possible. He dressed rapidly. The lift was not yet running, so he went up two flights of stairs and rang at their door. Cherry Beamish, in her dressing-gown, admitted him. From her face he knew, at once, — though her smile was almost radiant as she took his hand.

"Yes, it is over for her, poor dear," she said softly. "It must have happened in her sleep. I was with her until after midnight. When I went in

again, a little after five, I found her just as I want
you to see her now; before her maid comes, before anyone has been informed."

She led him on tiptoe into Gabrielle's chamber. The first shafts of the morning sunlight
slanted through the Venetian blinds. A blue
dressing-gown hung on a tall chair beside the bed,
blue slippers beneath it. Gabrielle lay on her
back, her eyes closed. The face that had outfaced
so many changes of fortune had no longer need
to muffle itself in furs, to shrink away from curious eyes, or harden itself into scorn. It lay on the
pillow regal, calm, victorious, — like an open con-
fession.

Seabury stood for a moment looking down at
her. Then he went to the window and peered out
through the open slats at the sun, come at last
over the mountains into a sky that had long been
blue: the same mountains they were driving
among yesterday.

Presently Cherry Beamish spoke to him. She
pointed to the hand that lay on the turned-back
sheet. "See how changed her hands are; like those

of a young woman. She forgot to take off her rings last night, or she was too tired. Yes, dear, you needed a long rest. And now you are with your own kind."

"I feel that, too, Chetty. She is with them. All is well. Thank you for letting me come." He stooped for a moment over the hand that had been gracious to his youth. They went out into the salon, carefully closing the door behind them.

"Now, my dear, stay here, with her. I will go to the management, and I will arrange all that must be done."

Some hours later, after he had gone through the formalities required by French law, Seabury encountered the three journalists in front of the hotel.

Next morning the great man from the Riviera to whom Seabury had telegraphed came in person, his car laden with flowers from his conservatories. He stood on the platform at the railway station, his white head uncovered, all the while that the box containing Gabrielle Longstreet's coffin was being carried across and put on the express. Then he shook Seabury's hand in farewell, and bent gallantly over Chetty's. Seabury and Chetty were going to Paris on that same express.

After her illness two years ago Gabrielle de Couçy had bought a lot *à perpétuité* in Père-La-chaise. That was rather a fashion then: Adelina Patti, Sarah Bernhardt, and other ladies who had once held a place in the world made the same choice.

THE BEST YEARS

THE BEST YEARS

I

On a bright September morning in the year 1899
Miss Evangeline Knightly was driving through
the beautiful Nebraska land which lies between
the Platte River and the Kansas line. She drove
slowly, for she loved the country, and she held
the reins loosely in her gloved hand. She drove
about a great deal and always wore leather gaunt-
lets. Her hands were small, well shaped and very
white, but they freckled in hot sunlight.

Miss Knightly was a charming person to meet

The Best Years

— and an unusual type in a new country: oval
face, small head delicately set (the oval chin tilting inward instead of the square chin thrust out) ,
hazel eyes, a little blue, a little green, tiny dots of
brown. . . . Somehow these splashes of colour
made light — and warmth. When she laughed,
her eyes positively glowed with humour, and in
each oval cheek a roguish dimple came magically
to the surface. Her laugh was delightful because
it was intelligent, discriminating, not the physical spasm which seizes children when they are
tickled, and growing boys and girls when they
are embarrassed. When Miss Knightly laughed,
it was apt to be because of some happy coinci-
dence or droll mistake. The farmers along the
road always felt flattered if they could make Miss
Knightly laugh. Her voice had as many colours as
her eyes — nearly always on the bright side,
though it had a beautiful gravity for people who
were in trouble.

It is only fair to say that in the community
where she lived Miss Knightly was considered an
intelligent young woman, but plain — distinctly

plain. The standard of female beauty seems to be the same in all newly settled countries: Australia, New Zealand, the farming country along the Platte. It is, and was, the glowing, smiling calendar girl sent out to advertise agricultural implements. Colour was everything, modelling was nothing. A nose was a nose — any shape would do; a forehead was the place where the hair stopped, chin utterly negligible unless it happened to be more than two inches long.

Miss Knightly's old mare, Molly, took her time along the dusty, sunflower-bordered roads that morning, occasionally pausing long enough to snatch off a juicy, leafy sunflower top in her yellow teeth. This she munched as she ambled along. Although Molly had almost the slowest trot in the world, she really preferred walking. Sometimes she fell into a doze and stumbled. Miss Knightly also, when she was abroad on these long drives, preferred the leisurely pace. She loved the beautiful autumn country; loved to look at it, to breathe it. She was not a "dreamy" person, but she was thoughtful and very observing. She relished the morning; the great blue of the sky, smiling, cloudless, — and the land that lay level as far as the eye could see. The horizon was like a perfect circle, a great embrace, and within it lay the cornfields, still green, and the yellow wheat stubble, miles and miles of it, and the pasture lands where the white-faced cattle led lives of utter content. All their movements were deliberate and dignified. They grazed through all the morning; approached their metal water tank and drank. If the windmill had run too long and the tank had overflowed, the cattle trampled the overflow into deep mud and cooled their feet. Then they drifted off to graze again. Grazing was not merely eating, it was also a pastime, a form of reflection, perhaps meditation.

Miss Knightly was thinking, as Molly jogged along, that the barbed-wire fences, though ugly in themselves, had their advantages. They did not cut the country up into patterns as did the rail fences and stone walls of her native New England. They were, broadly regarded, invisible — did not impose themselves upon the eye. She seemed to be driving through a fineless land. On her left the Hereford cattle apparently wandered at will: the tall sunflowers hid the wire that kept them off the road. Far away, on the horizon line, a troop of colts were galloping, all in the same direction — purely for exercise, one would say. Between her and the horizon the white wheels of windmills told her where the farmhouses sat.

Miss Knightly was abroad this morning with a special purpose — to visit country schools. She was the County Superintendent of Public Instruction. A grim title, that, to put upon a charming young woman. . . . Fortunately it was seldom used except on reports which she signed, and there it was usually printed. She was not even called "the Superintendent." A country schoolteacher said to her pupils: "I think Miss Knightly will come to see us this week. She was at Walnut Creek yesterday."

After she had driven westward through the pasture lands for an hour or so, Miss Knightly turned her mare north and very soon came into a rich farming district, where the fields were too valuable to be used for much grazing. Big red barns, rows of yellow straw stacks, green orchards, trim white farmhouses, fenced gardens.

Looking at her watch, Miss Knightly found that it was already after eleven o'clock. She touched Molly delicately with the whip and roused her to a jog trot. Presently they stopped before a little one-storey schoolhouse. All the windows were open. At the hitch-bar in the yard five horses were tethered — their saddles and bridles piled in an empty buckboard. There was a yard, but no fence — though on one side of the playground was a woven-wire fence covered with the vines of sturdy rambler roses — very pretty in the spring. It enclosed a cemetery — very few graves, very much sun and waving yellow grass, open to the singing from the schoolroom and the shouts of the boys playing ball at noon. The cemetery never depressed the children, and surely the school cast no gloom over the cemetery.

When Miss Knightly stopped before the door, a boy ran out to hand her from the buggy and to

take care of Molly. The little teacher stood on the
doorstep, her face lost, as it were, in a wide smile
of tremulous gladness.

Miss Knightly took her hand, held it for a moment and looked down into the child's face — she
was scarcely more — and said in the very gentlest
shade of her many-shaded voice, "Everything going well, Lesley?"

The teacher replied in happy little gasps, "Oh
yes, Miss Knightly! It's all so much easier than it
was last year. I have some such lovely children —
and they're all *good!*"

Miss Knightly took her arm, and they went
into the schoolroom. The pupils grinned a wel-
come to the visitor. The teacher asked the con-
ventional question: What recitation would she
like to hear?

Whatever came next in the usual order, Miss
Knightly said.

The class in geography came next. The children were "bounding" the States. When the
North Atlantic States had been disposed of with

more or less accuracy, the little teacher said they would now jump to the Middle West, to bring the lesson nearer home.

"Suppose we begin with Illinois. That is your State, Edward, so I will call on you."

A pale boy rose and came front of the class; a little fellow aged ten, maybe, who was plainly a newcomer — wore knee pants and stockings, instead of long trousers or blue overalls like the other boys. His hands were clenched at his sides, and he was evidently much frightened. Looking appealingly at the little teacher, he began in a high treble: "The State of Illinois is bounded on the north by Lake Michigan, on the east by Lake Michigan . . ." He felt he had gone astray, and language utterly failed. A quick shudder ran over him from head to foot, and an accident happened. His dark blue stockings grew darker still, and his knickerbockers very dark. He stood there as if nailed to the floor. The teacher went up to him and took his hand and led him to his desk.

"You're too tired, Edward," she said. "We're all tired, and it's almost noon. So you can all run

out and play, while I talk to Miss Knightly and
tell her how naughty you all are."

The children laughed (all but poor Edward),
laughed heartily, as if they were suddenly re-
lieved from some strain. Still laughing and punch-
ing each other they ran out into the sunshine.

Miss Knightly and the teacher (her name, by
the way, was Lesley Ferguesson) sat down on a
bench in the corner.

"I'm so sorry that happened, Miss Knightly. I
oughtn't to have called on him. He's so new here,
and he's a nervous little boy. I thought he'd like
to speak up for his State. He seems homesick."

"My dear, I'm glad you did call on him, and
I'm glad the poor little fellow had an accident, —
if he doesn't get too much misery out of it. The
way those children behaved astonished me. Not a
wink, or grin, or even a look. Not a wink from the
Haymaker boy. I watched him. His mother has
no such delicacy. They have just the best kind of
good manners. How do you do it, Lesley?"

Lesley gave a happy giggle and flushed as red
as a poppy. "Oh, I don't do anything! You see

they really *are* nice children. You remember last year I did have a little trouble — till they got used to me."

"But they all passed their finals, and one girl, who was older than her teacher, got a school."

"Hush, hush, ma'am! I'm afraid for the walls to hear it! Nobody knows our secret but my mother."

"I'm very well satisfied with the results of our crime, Lesley."

The girl blushed again. She loved to hear Miss Knightly speak her name, because she always sounded the *s* like a *z*, which made it seem gentler and more intimate. Nearly everyone else, even her mother, hissed the *s* as if it were spelled "Lessley." It was embarrassing to have such a queer name, but she respected it because her father had chosen it for her.

"Where are you going to stay all night, Miss Knightly?" she asked rather timidly.

"I think Mrs. Ericson expects me to stay with her."

"Mrs. Hunt, where I stay, would be awful glad

to have you, but I know you'll be more comfortable at Mrs. Ericson's. She's a lovely housekeeper." Lesley resigned the faint hope that Miss Knightly would stay where she herself boarded, and broke out eagerly:

"Oh, Miss Knightly, have you seen any of our boys lately? Mother's too busy to write to me often."

"Hector looked in at my office last week. He came to the Court House with a telegram for the sheriff. He seemed well and happy."

"Did he? But Miss Knightly, I wish he hadn't taken that messenger job. I hate so for him to quit school."

"Now, I wouldn't worry about that, my dear. School isn't everything. He'll be getting good experience every day at the depot."

"Do you think so? I haven't seen him since he went to work."

"Why, how long has it been since you were home?"

"It's over a month now. Not since my school started. Father has been working all our horses on

The Best Years

the farm. Maybe you can share my lunch with me?"

"I brought a lunch for the two of us, my dear. Call your favourite boy to go to my buggy and get my basket for us. After lunch I would like to hear the advanced arithmetic class."

While the pupils were doing their sums at the blackboard, Miss Knightly herself was doing a little figuring. This was Thursday. Tomorrow she would visit two schools, and she had planned to spend Friday night with a pleasant family on Farmers' Creek. But she could change her schedule and give this homesick child a visit with her family in the county seat. It would inconvenience her very little.

When the class in advanced arithmetic was dismissed, Miss Knightly made a joking little talk to the children and told them about a very bright little girl in Scotland who knew nearly a whole play of Shakespeare's by heart, but who wrote in her diary: "Nine times nine is the Devil"; which proved, she said, that there are two kinds of memory, and God is very good to anyone to whom he gives both kinds. Then she asked if the pupils might have a special recess of half an hour, as a present from her. They gave her a cheer and out they trooped, the boys to the ball ground, and the girls to the cemetery, to sit neatly on the headstones and discuss Miss Knightly.

During their recess the Superintendent disclosed her plan. "I've been wondering, Lesley, whether you wouldn't like to go back to town with me after school tomorrow. We could get into MacAlpin by seven o'clock, and you could have all of Saturday and Sunday at home. Then we would make an early start Monday morning, and I would drop you here at the schoolhouse at nine o'clock."

The little teacher caught her breath — she became quite pale for a moment.

"Oh Miss Knightly, could you? Could you?"

"Of course I can. I'll stop for you here at four o'clock tomorrow afternoon."

II

The dark secret between Lesley and Miss Knightly was that only this September had the girl reached the legal age for teachers, yet she had been teaching all last year when she was still under age!

Last summer, when the applicants for teachers' certificates took written examinations in the County Superintendent's offices at the Court House in MacAlpin, Lesley Ferguesson had appeared with some twenty-six girls and nine boys. She wrote all morning and all afternoon for two days. Miss Knightly found her paper one of the best in the lot. A week later, when all the papers were filed, Miss Knightly told Lesley she could certainly give her a school. The morning after she had thus notified Lesley, she found the girl herself waiting on the sidewalk in front of the house where Miss Knightly boarded.

"Could I walk over to the Court House with you, Miss Knightly? I ought to tell you something," she blurted out at once. "On that paper I didn't put down my real age. I put down sixteen, and I won't be fifteen until this September."

"But I checked you with the high-school records, Lesley."

"I know. I put it down wrong there, too. I didn't want to be the class baby, and I hoped I could get a school soon, to help out at home."

The County Superintendent thought she would long remember that walk to the Court House. She could see that the child had spent a bad night; and she had walked up from her home down by the depot, quite a mile away, probably without breakfast.

"If your age is wrong on both records, why do you tell me about it now?"

"Oh, Miss Knightly, I got to thinking about it last night, how if you did give me a school it might all come out, and mean people would say you knew about it and broke the law."

Miss Knightly was thoughtless enough to chuckle. "But, my dear, don't you see that if I didn't know about it until this moment, I am completely innocent?"

The Best Years

The child who was walking beside her stopped short and burst into sobs. Miss Knightly put her arm around those thin, eager, forward-reaching shoulders.

"Don't cry, dear. I was only joking. There's nothing very dreadful about it. You didn't give your age under oath, you know." The sobs didn't stop. "Listen, let me tell you something. That big Hatch boy put his age down as nineteen, and I know he was teaching down in Nemaha County four years ago. I can't always be sure about the age applicants put down. I have to use my judgment."

The girl lifted her pale, troubled face and murmured, "Judgment?"

"Yes. Some girls are older at thirteen than others are at eighteen. Your paper was one of the best handed in this year, and I am going to give you a school. Not a big one, but a nice one, in a nice part of the county. Now let's go into Ernie's coffee shop and have some more breakfast. You have a long walk home."

Of course, fourteen was rather young for a

teacher in an ungraded school, where she was likely to have pupils of sixteen and eighteen in her classes. But Miss Knightly's "judgment" was justified by the fact that in June the school directors of the Wild Rose district asked to have "Miss Ferguesson" back for the following year.

III

At four o'clock on Friday afternoon Miss Knightly stopped at the Wild Rose schoolhouse to find the teacher waiting by the roadside, and the pupils already scattering across the fields, their tin lunch pails flashing back the sun. Lesley was standing almost in the road itself, her grey "telescope" bag at her feet. The moment old Molly stopped, she stowed her bag in the back of the buggy and climbed in beside Miss Knightly. Her smile was so eager and happy that her friend chuckled softly. "You still get a little homesick, don't you, Lesley?"

She didn't deny it. She gave a guilty laugh and murmured, "I do miss the boys."

The afternoon sun was behind them, throwing

over the pastures and the harvested, resting fields
that wonderful light, so yellow that it is actually
orange. The three hours and the fourteen miles
seemed not overlong. As the buggy neared the
town of MacAlpin, Miss Knightly thought she
could feel Lesley's heart beat. The girl had been
silent a long while when she exclaimed:

"Look, there's the standpipe!"

The object of this emotion was a red sheet-iron
tube which thrust its naked ugliness some eighty
feet into the air and held the water supply for the
town of MacAlpin. As it stood on a hill, it was
the first thing one saw on approaching the town
from the west. Old Molly, too, seemed to have
spied this heartening landmark, for she quick-
ened her trot without encouragement from the
whip. From that point on, Lesley said not a word.
There were two more low hills (very low), and
then Miss Knightly turned off the main road and
drove by a short cut through the baseball ground,
to the south appendix of the town proper, the
"depot settlement" where the Ferguessons lived.

The Best Years

Their house stood on a steep hillside — a storey-and-a-half frame house with a basement on the downhill side, faced with brick up to the first-floor level. When the buggy stopped before the yard gate, two little boys came running out of the front door. Miss Knightly's passenger vanished from her side — she didn't know just when Lesley alighted. Her attention was distracted by the appearance of the mother, with a third boy, still in kilts, trotting behind her.

Mrs. Ferguesson was not a person who could be overlooked. All the merchants in MacAlpin admitted that she was a fine figure of a woman. As she came down the little yard and out of the gate, the evening breeze ruffled her wavy auburn hair. Her quick step and alert, upright carriage gave one the impression that she got things done. Coming up to the buggy, she took Miss Knightly's hand.

"Why, it's Miss Knightly! And she's brought our girl along to visit us. That was mighty clever of you, Miss, and these boys will surely be a

happy family. They do miss their sister." She
spoke clearly, distinctly, but with a slight Missouri turn of speech.

By this time Lesley and her brothers had become telepathically one. Miss Knightly couldn't
tell what the boys said to her, or whether they
said anything, but they had her old canvas bag
out of the buggy and up on the porch in no time
at all. Lesley ran toward the front door, hurried
back to thank Miss Knightly, and then disappeared, holding fast to the little chap in skirts.
She had forgotten to ask at what time Miss
Knightly would call for her on Monday, but her
mother attended to that. When Mrs. Ferguesson
followed the children through the hall and the
little back parlour into the dining-room, Lesley
turned to her and asked breathlessly, almost
sharply:

"Where's Hector?"

"He's often late on Friday night, dear. He telephoned me from the depot and said not to wait
supper for him — he'd get a sandwich at the

lunch counter. Now how *are* you, my girl?" Mrs. Ferguesson put her hands on Lesley's shoulders and looked into her glowing eyes.

"Just fine, Mother. I like my school so much! And the scholars are nicer even than they were last year. I just love some of them."

At this the little boy in kilts (the fashion of the times, though he was four years old) caught his sister's skirt in his two hands and jerked it to get her attention. "No, no!" he said mournfully, "you don't love anybody but us!"

His mother laughed, and Lesley stooped and gave him the tight hug he wanted.

The family supper was over. Mrs. Ferguesson put on her apron. "Sit right down, Lesley, and talk to the children. No, I won't let you help me. You'll help me most by keeping them out of my way. I'll scramble you an egg and fry you some ham, so sit right down in your own place. I have some stewed plums for your dessert, and a beautiful angel cake I bought at the Methodist bake sale. Your father's gone to some political meeting, so we had supper early. You'll be a nice surprise for him when he gets home. He hadn't been gone half an hour when Miss Knightly drove up. Sit still, dear, it only bothers me if anybody tries to help me. I'll let you wash the dishes afterward, like we always do."

Lesley sat down at the half-cleared table; an oval-shaped table which could be extended by the insertion of "leaves" when Mrs. Ferguesson had company. The room was already dusky (twilights are short in a flat country), and one of the boys switched on the light which hung by a cord high above the table. A shallow china shade over the bulb threw a glaring white light down on the sister and the boys who stood about her chair. Lesley wrinkled up her brow, but it didn't occur to her that the light was too strong. She gave herself up to the feeling of being at home. It went all through her, that feeling, like getting into a warm bath when one is tired. She was safe from everything, was where she wanted to be, where she ought to be. A plant that has been washed out by a rain storm feels like that, when a kind gardener puts it gently back into its own earth with its own group.

The two older boys, Homer and Vincent, kept interrupting each other, trying to tell her things, but she didn't really listen to what they said. The little fellow stood close beside her chair, holding on to her skirt, fingering the glass buttons on her jacket. He was named Bryan, for his father's hero, but he didn't fit the name very well. He was a rather wistful and timid child.

Mrs. Ferguesson brought the ham and eggs and the warmed-up coffee. Then she sat down opposite her daughter to watch her enjoy her supper. "Now don't talk to her, boys. Let her eat in peace."

Vincent spoke up. "Can't I just tell her what happened to my lame pigeon?"

Mrs. Ferguesson merely shook her head. She had control in that household, sure enough!

Before Lesley had quite finished her supper she heard the front door open and shut. The boys started up, but the mother raised a warning finger. They understood; a surprise. They were still as mice, and listened: A pause in the hall . . . he was hanging up his cap. Then he came in — the flower of the family.

For a moment he stood speechless in the doorway, the "incandescent" glaring full on his curly yellow hair and his amazed blue eyes. He was surprised indeed!

"Lesley!" he breathed, as if he were talking in his sleep.

She couldn't sit still. Without knowing that she got up and took a step, she had her arms around her brother. "It's me, Hector! Ain't I lucky? Miss Knightly brought me in."

"What time did you get here? You might have telephoned me, Mother."

"Dear, she ain't been here much more than half an hour."

"And Miss Knightly brought you in with old Molly, did she?" Oh, the lovely voice he had, that Hector! — warm, deliberate . . . it made the most commonplace remark full of meaning. He had to say merely that — and it told his appreciation of Miss Knightly's kindness, even a playful gratitude to Molly, her clumsy, fat, road-pounding old mare. He was tall for his age, was Hector, and he had the fair pink-cheeked complexion which Lesley should have had and didn't.

Mrs. Ferguesson rose. "Now let's all go into the parlour and talk. We'll come back and clear up afterward." With this she opened the folding doors, and they followed her and found comfortable chairs — there was even a home-made hassock for Bryan. There were real books in the sectional bookcases (old Ferg's fault), and there was a real Brussels carpet in soft colours on the floor. That was Lesley's fault. Most of her savings from her first year's teaching had gone into that carpet. She had chosen it herself from the samples which Marshall Field's travelling man brought to MacAlpin. There were comfortable old-fashioned pictures on the walls — "Venice by Moonlight" and such. Lesley and Hector thought it a beautiful room.

Of course the room was pleasant because of the feeling the children had for one another, and because in Mrs. Ferguesson there was authority and organization. Here the family sat and talked until Father came home. He was always treated a little like company. His wife and his children had a deep respect for him and for experimental farming, and profound veneration for William Jennings Bryan. Even little Bryan knew he was named for a great man, and must some day stop being afraid of the dark.

James Grahame Ferguesson was a farmer. He spent most of his time on what he called an "experimental farm." (The neighbours had other names for it — some of them amusing.) He was a loosely built man; had drooping shoulders carried with a forward thrust. He was a ready speaker, and usually made the Fourth of July speech in MacAlpin — spoke from a platform in the Court House grove, and even the farmers who joked about Ferguesson came to hear him. Alf Delaney declared: "I like to see anything done well — even talking. If old Ferg could shuck corn as fast as he can rustle the dictionary, I'd hire him, even if he is a Pop."

The Best Years

Old Ferg was not at all old — just turned forty — but he was fussy about the spelling of his name. He wrote it James Ferguesson. The merchants, even the local newspaper, simply would not spell it that way. They left letters out, or they put letters in. He complained about this repeatedly, and the result was that he was simply called "Ferg" to his face, and "old Ferg" to his back. His neighbours, both in town and in the country where he farmed, liked him because he gave them so much to talk about. He couldn't keep a hired man long at any wages. His habits were too unconventional. He rose early, saw to the chores like any other man, and went into the field for the morning. His lunch was a cold spread from his wife's kitchen, reinforced by hot tea. (The hired man was expected to bring his own lunch — outrageous!) After lunch Mr. Ferguesson took off his boots and lay down on the blue gingham sheets of a wide bed, and remained there until what he called "the cool of the afternoon." When that refreshing season arrived, he fed and watered his work horses, put the young gelding to his buckboard, and drove four miles to MacAlpin for his wife's hot supper. Mrs. Ferguesson, though not at all a meek woman or a stupid one, unquestioningly believed him when he told her that he did his best thinking in the afternoon. He hinted to her that he was working out in his head something that would benefit the farmers of the county more than all the corn and wheat they could raise even in a good year.

Sometimes Ferguesson did things she regretted — not because they were wrong, but because other people had mean tongues. When a fashion came in for giving names to farms which had hitherto been designated by figures (range, section, quarter, etc.), and his neighbours came out with "Lone Tree Farm," "Cold Spring Farm," etc., Ferguesson tacked on a cottonwood tree by his gate a neatly painted board inscribed: WIDE AWAKE FARM.

His neighbours, who could never get used to his afternoon siesta, were not long in converting this prophetic christening into "Hush-a-bye Farm." Mrs. Ferguesson overheard some of this joking on a Saturday night (she was marketing late after a lodge meeting on top of a busy day), and she didn't like it. On Sunday morning when he was dressing for church, she asked her husband why he ever gave the farm such a foolish name. He explained to her that the important crop on that farm was an idea. His farm was like an observatory where one watched the signs of the times and saw the great change that was coming for the benefit of all mankind. He even quoted Tennyson about looking into the future "far as human eye could see." It had been a long time since he had quoted any poetry to her. She sighed and dropped the matter.

On the whole, Ferg did himself a good turn when he put up that piece of nomenclature. People drove out of their way for miles to see it. They felt more kindly toward old Ferg because he wrote himself down such an ass. In a hard-working farming community a good joke is worth something. Ferguesson himself felt a gradual warming toward him among his neighbours. He ascribed it to the power of his oratory. It was really because he had made himself so absurd, but this he never guessed. Idealists are seldom afraid of ridicule — if they recognize it.

The Ferguesson children believed that their father was misunderstood by people of inferior intelligence, and that conviction gave them a "cause" which bound them together. They must do better than other children; better in school, and better on the playground. They must turn in a quarter of a dollar to help their mother out whenever they could. Experimental farming wasn't immediately remunerative.

Fortunately there was never any rent to pay. They owned their house down by the depot. When Mrs. Ferguesson's father died down in Missouri, she bought that place with what he left her. She knew that was the safe thing to do, her husband being a thinker. Her children were bound to her, and to that house, by the deepest, the most solemn loyalty. They never spoke of that covenant to each other, never even formulated it in their own minds — never. It was a consciousness they shared, and it gave them a family complexion.

On this Saturday of Lesley's surprise visit home, Father was with the family for breakfast. That was always a pleasant way to begin the day — especially on Saturday, when no one was in a hurry. He had grave good manners toward his wife and his children. He talked to them as if they were grown-up, reasonable beings — talked a trifle as if from a rostrum, perhaps, — and he never indulged in small-town gossip. He was much more likely to tell them what he had read in the *Omaha World-Herald* yesterday; news of the State capital and the national capital. Sometimes he told them what a grasping, selfish country England was. Very often he explained to them how the gold standard had kept the poor man down. The family seldom bothered him about petty matters — such as that Homer needed new shoes, or that the iceman's bill for the whole summer had come in for the third time. Mother would take care of that.

On this particular Saturday morning Ferguesson gave especial attention to Lesley. He asked her about her school, and had her name her pupils. "I think you are fortunate to have the Wild Rose school, Lesley," he said as he rose from the table. "The farmers up there are open-minded and prosperous. I have sometimes wished that I had settled up there, though there are certain advantages in living at the county seat. The educational opportunities are better. Your friendship with Miss Knightly has been a broadening influence."

He went out to hitch up the buckboard to drive to the farm, while his wife put up the lunch he was to take along with him, and Lesley went upstairs to make the beds.

"Upstairs" was a story in itself, a secret romance. No caller or neighbour had ever been allowed to go up there. All the children loved it — it was their very own world where there were no older people poking about to spoil things. And it was unique — not at all like other people's upstairs chambers. In her stuffy little bedroom out

in the country Lesley had more than once cried
for it.

Lesley and the boys liked space, not tight cub-
byholes. Their upstairs was a long attic which
ran the whole length of the house, from the front
door downstairs to the kitchen at the back. Its
great charm was that it was unlined. No plaster,
no beaver-board lining; just the roof shingles, supported by long, unplaned, splintery rafters that
sloped from the sharp roof-peak down to the floor
of the attic. Bracing these long roof rafters were
cross rafters on which one could hang things — a
little personal washing, a curtain for tableaux, a
rope swing for Bryan.

In this spacious, undivided loft were two brick
chimneys, going up in neat little stair-steps from
the plank floor to the shingle roof — and out of
it to the stars! The chimneys were of red, un-
glazed brick, with lines of white mortar to hold
them together.

Last year, after Lesley first got her school, Mrs.
Ferguesson exerted her authority and partitioned
off a little room over the kitchen end of the "up-

stairs" for her daughter. Before that, all the children slept in this delightful attic. The three older boys occupied two wide beds, their sister her little single bed. Bryan, subject to croup, still slumbered downstairs near his mother, but he looked forward to his ascension as to a state of pure beatitude.

There was certainly room enough up there for widely scattered quarters, but the three beds stood in a row, as in a hospital ward. The children liked to be close enough together to share experiences.

Experiences were many. Perhaps the most exciting was when the driving, sleety snowstorms came on winter nights. The roof shingles were old and had curled under hot summer suns. In a driving snowstorm the frozen flakes sifted in through all those little cracks, sprinkled the beds and the children, melted on their faces, in their hair! That was delightful. The rest of you was snug and warm under blankets and comforters, with a hot brick at one's feet. The wind howled outside; sometimes the white light from the snow and the half-strangled moon came in through the single end window. Each child had his own dream-adventure. They did not exchange confidences; every "fellow" had a right to his own. They never told their love.

If they turned in early, they had a good while to enjoy the outside weather; they never went to sleep until after ten o'clock, for then came the sweetest morsel of the night. At that hour Number Seventeen, the westbound passenger, whistled in. The station and the engine house were perhaps an eighth of a mile down the hill, and from far away across the meadows the children could hear that whistle. Then came the heavy pants of the locomotive in the frosty air. Then a hissing — then silence: she was taking water.

On Saturdays the children were allowed to go down to the depot to see Seventeen come in. It was a fine sight on winter nights. Sometimes the great locomotive used to sweep in armoured in ice and snow, breathing fire like a dragon, its great red eye shooting a blinding beam along the white roadbed and shining wet rails. When it stopped, it panted like a great beast. After it was watered by the big hose from the overhead tank, it seemed to draw long deep breaths, ready to charge afresh over the great Western land.

Yes, they were grand old warriors, those towering locomotives of other days. They seemed to mean power, conquest, triumph — Jim Hill's dream. They set children's hearts beating from Chicago to Los Angeles. They were the awakeners of many a dream.

As she made the boys' beds that Saturday morning and put on clean sheets, Lesley was thinking she would give a great deal to sleep out here as she used to. But when she got her school last year, her mother had said she must have a room of her own. So a carpenter brought sheathing and "lined" the end of the long loft — the end over the kitchen; and Mrs. Ferguesson bought a little yellow washstand and a bowl and pitcher, and said with satisfaction: "Now you see, Lesley, if you were sick, we would have some place to take the doctor." To be sure, the doctor would

have to be admitted through the kitchen, and
then come up a dark winding stairway with two
turns. (Mr. Ferguesson termed it "the turnpike."
His old Scotch grandmother, he said, had always
thus called a winding stairway.) And Lesley's
room, when you got there, was very like a snug
wooden box. It was possible, of course, to leave
her door open into the long loft, where the wood
was brown and the chimneys red and the weather
always so close to one. Out there things were still
wild and rough — it wasn't a bedroom or a chamber — it was a hall, in the old baronial sense, reminded her of the lines in their *Grimm's Fairy
Tales* book:

> Return, return, thou youthful bride,
> This is a robbers' hall inside.

IV

When her daughter had put the attic to rights,
Mrs. Ferguesson went uptown to do her Saturday marketing. Lesley slipped out through the
kitchen door and sat down on the back porch.
The front porch was kept neat and fit to receive

callers, but the back porch was given over to the
boys. It was a messy-looking place, to be sure.
From the wooden ceiling hung two trapezes. At
one corner four boxing gloves were piled in a
broken chair. In the trampled, grassless back yard,
two-by-fours, planted upright, supported a length
of lead pipe on which Homer practised bar exercises. Lesley sat down on the porch floor, her feet
on the ground, and sank into idleness and safety
and perfect love.

The boys were much the dearest things in the
world to her. To love them so much was just . . .
happiness. To think about them was the most
perfect form of happiness. Had they been actually present, swinging on the two trapezes, turning on the bar, she would have been too much
excited, too actively happy to be perfectly happy.
But sitting in the warm sun, with her feet on the
good ground, even her mother away, she almost
ceased to exist. The feeling of being at home was
complete, absolute: it made her sleepy. And that
feeling was not so much the sense of being pro-

tected by her father and mother as of being with, and being one with, her brothers. It was the clan feeling, which meant life or death for the blood, not for the individual. For some reason, or for no reason, back in the beginning, creatures wanted the blood to continue.

After the noonday dinner Mrs. Ferguesson thoughtfully confided to her daughter while they were washing the dishes:

"Lesley, I'm divided in my mind. I would so appreciate a quiet afternoon with you, but I've a sort of engagement with the P.E.O. A lady from Canada is to be there to talk to us, and I've promised to introduce her. And just when I want to have a quiet time with you."

Lesley gave a sigh of relief and thought how fortunate it is that circumstances do sometimes make up our mind for us. In that battered canvas bag upstairs there was a roll of arithmetic papers and "essays" which hung over her like a threat. Now she would have a still hour in their beauti-

ful parlour to correct them; the shades drawn
down, just enough light to read by, her father's
unabridged at hand, and the boys playing bat and
pitch in the back yard.

Lesley and her brothers were proud of their
mother's good looks, and that she never allowed
herself to become a household drudge, as so many
of her neighbours did. She "managed," and the
boys helped her to manage. For one thing, there
were never any dreary tubs full of washing standing about, and there was no ironing day to make
a hole in the week. They sent all the washing,
even the sheets, to the town steam laundry. Hector, with his weekly wages as messenger boy,
and Homer and Vincent with their stable jobs,
paid for it. That simple expedient did away
with the worst blight of the working man's
home.

Mrs. Ferguesson was "public-spirited," and she
was the friend of all good causes. The business
men of the town agreed that she had a great deal
of influence, and that her name added strength to
any committee. She was generally spoken of as a

very *practical* woman, with an emphasis which implied several things. She was a "joiner," too! She was a Royal Neighbor, and a Neighborly Neighbor, and a P.E.O., and an Eastern Star. She had even joined the Methodist Win-a-Couple, though she warned them that she could not attend their meetings, as she liked to spend some of her evenings at home.

Promptly at six thirty Monday morning Miss Knightly's old mare stopped in front of the Ferguessons' house. The four boys were all on the front porch. James himself carried Lesley's bag down and put it into the buggy. He thanked the Superintendent very courteously for her kindness and kissed his daughter good-bye.

It had been at no trifling sacrifice that Miss Knightly was able to call for Lesley at six thirty. Customarily she started on her long drives at nine o'clock. This morning she had to give an extra half-dollar to the man who came to curry and harness her mare. She herself got no proper breakfast, but a cold sandwich and a cup of coffee at the station lunch counter — the only eating-place open at six o'clock. Most serious of all, she must push Molly a little on the road, to land her passenger at the Wild Rose schoolhouse at nine o'clock. Such small inconveniences do not sum up to an imposing total, but we assume them only for persons we really care for.

v

It was Christmas Eve. The town was busy with Christmas "exercises," and all the churches were lit up. Hector Ferguesson was going slowly up the hill which separated the depot settlement from the town proper. He walked at no messenger-boy pace tonight, crunching under his feet the snow which had fallen three days ago, melted, and then frozen hard. His hands were in the pockets of his new overcoat, which was so long that it almost touched the ground when he toiled up the steepest part of the hill. It was very heavy and not very warm. In those days there was a theory that in topcoats very little wool was necessary if they were woven tight enough and hard enough to "keep out the cold." A barricade was the idea. Hector carried the weight and clumsiness bravely, proudly. His new overcoat was a Christmas present from his sister. She had gone to the big town in the next county to shop for it, and bought it with her own money. He was thinking how kind Lesley was, and how hard she had worked for that money, and how much she had to put up with in the rough farmhouse where she boarded, out in the country. It was usually a poor housekeeper who was willing to keep a teacher, since they paid so little. Probably the amount Lesley spent for that coat would have kept her at a comfortable house all winter. When he grew up, and made lots of money (a brakeman — maybe an engineer), he would certainly be good to his sister.

Hector was a strange boy; a blend of the soft and the hard. In action he was practical, executive, like his mother. But in his mind, in his thoughts and plans, he was extravagant, often absurd. His mother suspected that he was "dreamy." Tonight, as he trailed up the frozen

wooden sidewalk toward the town, he kept looking up at the stars, which were unusually bright,
as they always seem over a stretch of snow. He
was wondering if there were angels up there,
watching the world on Christmas Eve. They came
before, on the first Christmas Eve, he knew.
Perhaps they kept the Anniversary. He thought
about a beautiful coloured picture tacked up in
Lesley's bedroom; two angels with white robes
and long white wings, flying toward a low hill
in the early dawn before sunrise, and on that
distant hill, against the soft daybreak light, were
three tiny crosses. He never doubted angels
looked like that. He was credulous and truthful
by nature. There was that look in his blue eyes.
He would get it knocked out of him, his mother
knew. But she believed he would always keep
some of it — enough to make him open-handed
and open-hearted.

Tonight Hector had his leather satchel full
of Christmas telegrams. After he had delivered
them all, he would buy his presents for his
mother and the children. The stores sold off

their special Christmas things at a discount after
eleven o'clock on Christmas Eve.

VI

Miss Knightly was in Lincoln, attending a
convention of Superintendents of Public Instruction, when the long-to-be-remembered blizzard
swept down over the prairie State. Travel and
telephone service were discontinued. A Chicago
passenger train was stalled for three days in a
deep cut west of W—. There she lay, and the
dining-car had much ado to feed the passengers.
Miss Knightly was snowbound in Lincoln.
She tarried there after the convention was dismissed and her fellow superintendents had gone
home to their respective counties. She was caught
by the storm because she had stayed over to see
Julia Marlowe (then young and so fair!) in *The
Love Chase*. She was not inconsolable to be de-
layed for some days. Why worry? She was staying at a small but very pleasant hotel, where the
food was good and the beds were comfortable.
She was New England born and bred, too con-

scientious to stay over in the city from mere self-indulgence, but quite willing to be lost to MacAlpin and X— County by the intervention of fate. She stayed, in fact, a week, greatly enjoying such luxuries as plenty of running water, hot baths, and steam heat. At that date MacAlpin houses, and even her office in the Court House, were heated by hard-coal stoves.

At last she was jogging home on a passenger train which left Lincoln at a convenient hour (it was two hours late, travel was still disorganized), when she was pleased to see Mr. Redman in conductor's uniform come into the car. Two of his boys had been her pupils when she taught in high school, before she was elected to a county office. Mr. Redman also seemed pleased, and after he had been through the train to punch tickets, he came back and sat down in the green plush seat opposite Miss Knightly and began to "tease."

"I hear there was a story going up at the Court House that you'd eloped. I was hoping you hadn't made a mistake."

"No. I thought it over and avoided the mistake. But what about you, Mr. Redman? You belong on the run west out of MacAlpin, don't you?"

"I don't know where I belong, Ma'm, and nobody else does. This is Jack Kelly's run, but he got his leg broke trying to help the train crew shovel the sleeping-car loose in that deep cut out of W—. The passengers were just freezing. This blizzard has upset everything. There's got to be better organization from higher up. This has taught us we just can't handle an emergency. Hard on stock, hard on people. A little neighbour of ours — why, you must know her, she was one of your teachers — Jim Ferguesson's little girl. She got pneumonia out there in the country and died out there."

Miss Knightly went so white that Redman without a word hurried to the end of the car and brought back a glass of water. He kept muttering that he was sorry . . . that he "always put his foot in it."

She did not disappoint him. She came back

quickly. "That's all right, Mr. Redman. I'd rather hear it before I get home. Did she get lost in the storm? I don't understand."

Mr. Redman sat down and did the best he could to repair damages.

"No, Ma'm, little Lesley acted very sensible, didn't lose her head. You see, the storm struck us about three o'clock in the afternoon. The whole day it had been mild and soft, like spring. Then it came down instanter, like a thousand tons of snow dumped out of the sky. My wife was out in the back yard taking in some clothes she'd hung to dry. She hadn't even a shawl over her head. The suddenness of it confused her so (she couldn't see three feet before her), she wandered around in our back yard, couldn't find her way back to the house. Pretty soon our old dog — he's part shepherd — came yappin' and whinin'. She dropped the clothes and held onto his hair, and he got her to the back porch. That's how bad it was in MacAlpin."

"And Lesley?" Miss Knightly murmured.

"Yes, Ma'm! I'm coming to that. Her scholars

tell about how the schoolroom got a little dark, and they all looked out, and there was no graveyard, and no horses that some of them had rode to school on. The boys jumped up to run out and see after the horses, but Lesley stood with her back against the door and wouldn't let 'em go out. Told 'em it would be over in a few minutes. Well, you see it wasn't. Over four feet of snow fell in less'n an hour. About six o'clock some of the fathers of the children that lived aways off started out on horseback, but the horses waded belly-deep, and a wind come up and it turned cold.

"Ford Robertson is the nearest neighbour, you know, — scarcely more than across the road — eighth of a mile, maybe. As soon as he come in from his corral — the Herefords had all bunched up together, over a hundred of 'em, under the lee of a big haystack, and he knew they wouldn't freeze. As soon as he got in, the missus made him go over to the schoolhouse an' take a rope along an' herd 'em all over to her house, teacher an' all, with the boys leading their horses. That night

Mrs. Robertson cooked nearly everything in the house for their supper, and she sent Ford upstairs to help Lesley make shakedown beds on the floor. Mrs. Robertson remembers when the big supper was ready and the children ate like wolves, Lesley didn't eat much — said she had a little headache. Next morning she was pretty sick. That day all the fathers came on horseback for the children. Robertson got one of them to go for old Doctor Small, and he came down on his horse. Doctor said it was pneumonia, and there wasn't much he could do. She didn't seem to have strength to rally. She was out of her head when he got there. She was mostly unconscious for three days, and just slipped out. The funeral is tomorrow. The roads are open now. They were to bring her home today."

The train stopped at a station, and Mr. Redman went to attend to his duties. When he next came through the car Miss Knightly spoke to him. She had recovered herself. Her voice was steady, though very low and very soft when she asked him:

"Were any of her family out there with her when she was ill?"

"Why, yes, Mrs. Ferguesson was out there. That boy Hector got his mother through, before the roads were open. He'd stop at a farmhouse and explain the situation and borrow a team and get the farmer or one of his hands to give them a lift to the next farm, and there they'd get a lift a little further. Everybody knew about the school and the teacher by that time, and wanted to help, no matter how bad the roads were. You see, Miss Knightly, everything would have gone better if it hadn't come on so freezing cold, and if the snow hadn't been so darn soft when it first fell. That family are terrible broke up. We all are, down at the depot. She didn't recognize them when they got there, I heard."

VII

Twenty years after that historic blizzard Evangeline Knightly — now Mrs. Ralph Thorndike — alighted from the fast eastbound passenger at the MacAlpin station. No one at the station knew who she was except the station master, and he was not quite sure. She looked older, but she also looked more prosperous, more worldly. When she approached him at his office door and asked, "Isn't this Mr. Beardsley?" he recognized her voice and speech.

"That's who. And it's my guess this is, or used to be, Miss Knightly. I've been here almost forever. No ambition. But you left us a long time ago. You're looking fine, Ma'm, if I may say so."

She thanked him and asked him to recommend a hotel where she could stay for a day or two.

He scratched his head. "Well, the Plummer House ain't no Waldorf-Astoria, but the travelling men give a good report of it. The Bishop always stays there when he comes to town. You like me to telephone for an otto [automobile] to take you up? Lord, when you left here there wasn't an otto in the town!"

Mrs. Thorndike smiled. "Not many in the world, I think. And can you tell me, Mr. Beardsley, where the Ferguessons live?"

"The depot Ferguessons? Oh, they live uptown

now. Ferg built right west of the Court House, right next to where the Donaldsons used to live. You'll find lots of changes. Some's come up, and some's come down. We used to laugh at Ferg and tell him politics didn't bring in the bacon. But he's got it on us now. The Democrats are sure grand job-givers. Throw 'em round for value received. I still vote the Republican ticket. Too old to change. Anyhow, all those new jobs don't affect the railroads much. They can't put a college professor on to run trains. Now I'll telephone for an otto for you."

Miss Knightly, after going to Denver, had married a very successful young architect, from New England, like herself, and now she was on her way back to Brunswick, Maine, to revisit the scenes of her childhood. Although she had never been in MacAlpin since she left it fifteen years ago, she faithfully read the MacAlpin *Messenger* and knew the important changes in the town.

After she had settled her room at the hotel, and unpacked her toilet articles, she took a card-

board box she had brought with her in the sleeping-car, and went out on a personal errand. She
came back to the hotel late for lunch — had a
tray sent up to her room, and at four o'clock
went to the office in the Court House which used
to be her office. This was the autumn of the
year, and she had a great desire to drive out
among the country schools and see how much
fifteen years had changed the land, the pupils,
the teachers.

When she introduced herself to the present
incumbent, she was cordially received. The young
Superintendent seemed a wide-awake, breezy
girl, with bobbed blond hair and crimson lips.
Her name was Wanda Bliss.

Mrs. Thorndike explained that her stay would
not be long enough to let her visit all the country
schools, but she would like Miss Bliss's advice as
to which were the most interesting.

"Oh, I can run you around to nearly all of
them in a day, in my car!"

Mrs. Thorndike thanked her warmly. She
liked young people who were not in the least

afraid of life or luck or responsibility. In her own youth there were very few like that. The teachers, and many of the pupils out in the country schools, were eager — but anxious. She laughed and told Miss Bliss that she meant to hire a buggy, if there was such a thing left in MacAlpin, and drive out into the country alone.

"I get you. You want to put on an old-home act. You might phone around to any farmers you used to know. Some of them still keep horses for haying."

Mrs. Thorndike got a list of the country teachers and the districts in which they taught. A few of them had been pupils in the schools she used to visit. Those she was determined to see.

The following morning she made the call she had stopped off at MacAlpin to make. She rang the doorbell at the house pointed out to her, and through the open window heard a voice call: "Come in, come in, please. I can't answer the bell."

Mrs. Thorndike opened the door into a shining oak hall with a shining oak stairway.

"Come right through, please. I'm in the back parlour. I sprained my ankle and can't walk yet."

The visitor followed the voice and found Mrs. Ferguesson sitting in a spring rocker, her bandaged right foot resting on a low stool.

"Come in, Ma'm. I have a bad sprain, and the little girl who does for me is downtown marketing. Maybe you came to see Mr. Ferguesson, but his office is — " here she broke off and looked up sharply — intently — at her guest. When the guest smiled, she broke out: "Miss Knightly! *Are* you Miss Knightly? Can it be?"

"They call me Mrs. Thorndike now, but I'm Evangeline Knightly just the same." She put out her hand, and Mrs. Ferguesson seized it with both her own.

"It's too good to be true!" she gasped with tears in her voice, "just too good to be true. The things we dream about that way don't happen." She held fast to Mrs. Thorndike's hand as if she were afraid she might vanish. "When did you come to town, and why didn't they let me know!"

The Best Years

"I came only yesterday, Mrs. Ferguesson, and I wanted to slip in on you just like this, with no one else around."

"Mr. Ferguesson must have known. But his mind is always off on some trail, and he never brings me any news when I'm laid up like this. Dear me! It's a long time." She pressed the visitor's hand again before she released it. "Get yourself a comfortable chair, dear, and sit down by me. I do hate to be helpless like this. It wouldn't have happened but for those slippery front stairs. Mr. Ferguesson just wouldn't put a carpet on them, because he says folks don't carpet hardwood stairs, and I tried to answer the doorbell in a hurry, and this is what come of it. I'm not naturally a clumsy woman on my feet."

Mrs. Thorndike noticed an aggrieved tone in her talk which had never been there in the old days when she had so much to be aggrieved about. She brought a chair and sat down close to Mrs. Ferguesson, facing her. The good woman had not changed much, she thought. There was a little grey in her crinkly auburn hair, and there were lines about her mouth which used not to be there, but her eyes had all the old fire.

"How comfortably you are fixed here, Mrs. Ferguesson! I'm so glad to find you like this."

"Yes, we're comfortable — now that they're all gone! It's mostly his taste. He took great interest." She spoke rather absently, and kept looking out through the polished hall toward the front door, as if she were expecting someone. It seemed a shame that anyone naturally so energetic should be enduring this foolish antiquated method of treating a sprain. The chief change in her, Mrs. Thorndike thought, was that she had grown softer. She reached for the visitor's hand again and held it fast. Tears came to her eyes.

Mrs. Thorndike ventured that she had found the town much changed for the better.

Yes, Mrs. Ferguesson supposed it was.

Then Mrs. Thorndike began in earnest. "How wonderful it is that all your sons have turned out so well! I take the MacAlpin paper chiefly to keep track of the Ferguesson boys. You and Mr. Ferguesson must be very proud."

"Yes'm, we are. We are thankful."

"Even the Denver papers have long articles about Hector and Homer and their great sheep ranches in Wyoming. And Vincent has become such a celebrated chemist, and is helping to destroy all the irreducible elements that I learned when I went to school. And Bryan is with Marshall Field!"

Mrs. Ferguesson nodded and pressed her hand, but she still kept looking down the hall toward the front door. Suddenly she turned with all herself to Mrs. Thorndike and with a storm of tears cried out from her heart: "Oh, Miss Knightly, talk to me about my Lesley! Seems so many have forgot her, but I know you haven't."

"No, Mrs. Ferguesson, I never forget her. Yesterday morning I took a box of roses that I brought with me from my own garden down to where she sleeps. I was glad to find a little seat there, so that I could stay for a long while and think about her."

"Oh, I wish I could have gone with you, Miss Knightly! (I can't call you anything else.) I wish we could have gone together. I can't help feeling she knows. *Anyhow*, we know! And there's nothing in all my life so precious to me to remember and think about as my Lesley. I'm no soft woman, either. The boys will tell you that. They'll tell you they got on because I always had a firm hand over them. They're all true to Lesley, my boys. Every time they come home they go down there. They feel it like I do, as if it had happened yesterday. Their father feels it, too, when he's not taken up with his abstractions. Anyhow, I don't think men feel things like women and boys. My boys have stayed boys. I do believe they feel as bad as I do about moving up here. We have four nice bedrooms upstairs to make them comfortable, should they all come home at once, and they're polite about us and tell us how well fixed we are. But Miss Knightly, I know at the bottom of their hearts they wish they was back in the old house down by the depot, sleeping in the attic."

Mrs. Thorndike stroked her hand. "I looked

for the old house as I was coming up from the station. I made the driver stop."

"Ain't it dreadful, what's been done to it? If I'd foreseen, I'd never have let Mr. Ferguesson sell it. It was in my name. I'd have kept it to go back to and remember sometimes. Folks in middle age make a mistake when they think they can better themselves. They can't, not if they have any heart. And the other kind don't matter — they aren't real people — just poor put-ons, that try to be like the advertisements. Father even took me to California one winter. I was miserable all the time. And there were plenty more like me — miserable underneath. The women lined up in cafeterias, carrying their little trays — like convicts, seemed to me — and running to beauty shops to get their poor old hands manicured. And the old men, Miss Knightly, I pitied them most of all! Old bent-backed farmers, standing round in their shirt-sleeves, in plazas and alleyways, pitching horseshoes like they used to do at home. I tell you, people are happiest where they've had their children and struggled along and been real folks, and not tourists. What do you think about all this running around, Miss Knightly? You're an educated woman, I never had much schooling."

"I don't think schooling gives people any wisdom, Mrs. Ferguesson. I guess only life does that."

"Well, this I know: our best years are when we're working hardest and going right ahead when we can hardly see our way out. Times I was a good deal perplexed. But I always had one comfort. I did own our own house. I never had to worry about the rent. Don't it seem strange to you, though, that all our boys are so practical, and their father such a dreamer?"

Mrs. Thorndike murmured that some people think boys are most likely to take after their mother.

Mrs. Ferguesson smiled absently and shook her head. Presently she came out with: "It's a comfort to me up here, on a still night I can still hear the trains whistle in. Sometimes, when

I can't sleep, I lie and listen for them. And I can almost think I am down there, with my children up in the loft. We were very happy." She looked up at her guest and smiled bravely. "I suppose you go away tonight?"

Mrs. Thorndike explained her plan to spend a day in the country.

"You're going out to visit the little schools? Why, God bless you, dear! You're still our Miss Knightly! But you'd better take a car, so you can get up to the Wild Rose school and back in one day. Do go there! The teacher is Mandy Perkins — she was one of her little scholars. You'll like Mandy, an' she loved Lesley. You must get Bud Sullivan to drive you. Engage him right now — the telephone's there in the hall, and the garage is 306. He'll creep along for you, if you tell him. He does for me. I often go out to the Wild Rose school, and over to see dear Mrs. Robertson, who ain't so young as she was then. I can't go with Mr. Ferguesson. He drives so fast it's no satisfaction. And then he's not always mindful. He's had some accidents. When he gets to thinking, he's just as likely to run down a cow as not. He's had to pay for one. You know cows will cross the road right in front of a car. Maybe their grandchildren calves will be more modern-minded."

Mrs. Thorndike did not see her old friend again, but she wrote her a long letter from Wiscasset, Maine, which Mrs. Ferguesson sent to her son Hector, marked, "To be returned, but first pass on to your brothers."

BEFORE BREAKFAST

BEFORE BREAKFAST

Henry Grenfell, of Grenfell & Saunders, got re-
sentfully out of bed after a bad night. The first
sleepless night he had ever spent in his own cabin,
on his own island, where nobody knew that he
was senior partner of Grenfell & Saunders, and
where the business correspondence was never for-
warded to him. He slipped on a blanket dressing-
gown over his pyjamas (island mornings in the
North Atlantic are chill before dawn), went to
the front windows of his bedroom, and ran up
the heavy blue shades which shut out the shame-

less blaze of the sunrise if one wanted to sleep late — and he usually did on the first morning after arriving. (The trip up from Boston was long and hard, by trains made up of the cast-off coaches of liquidated railroads, and then by the two worst boats in the world.) The cabin modestly squatted on a tiny clearing between a tall spruce wood and the sea, — sat about fifty yards back from the edge of the red sandstone cliff which dropped some two hundred feet to a narrow beach — so narrow that it was covered at high tide. The cliffs rose sheer on this side of the island, were undercut in places, and faced the east.

The east was already lightening; a deep red streak burnt over the sky-line water, and the water itself was thick and dark, indigo blue — occasionally a silver streak, where the tide was going out very quietly. While Grenfell stood at his window, a big snowshoe hare ran downhill from the spruce wood, bounded into the grass plot at the front door, and began nervously nibbling the clover.

He was puzzled and furtive; his jaws quivered, and his protruding eyes kept watch behind him as well as before. Grenfell was sure it was the hare that used to come every morning two summers ago and had become quite friendly. But now he seemed ill at ease; presently he started, sat still for an instant, then scampered up the grassy hillside and disappeared into the dark spruce wood. Silly thing! Still, it was a kind of greeting.

Grenfell left the window and went to his walnut washstand (no plumbing) and mechanically prepared to take a shower in the shed room behind his sleeping-chamber. He began his morning routine, still thinking about the hare.

First came the eye-drops. Tilting his head back, thus staring into the eastern horizon, he raised the glass dropper, but he didn't press the bulb. He saw something up there. While he was watching the rabbit the sky had changed. Above the red streak on the water line the sky had lightened to faint blue, and across the horizon a drift of fleecy rose cloud was floating. And through it a white-bright, gold-bright planet was shining. The morning star, of course. At this hour, and so near the sun, it would be Venus.

Behind her rose-coloured veils, quite alone in the sky already blue, she seemed to wait. She had come in on her beat, taken her place in the figure. Serene, impersonal splendour. Merciless perfection, ageless sovereignty. The poor hare and his clover, poor Grenfell and his eye-drops!

He braced himself against his washstand and still stared up at her. Something roused his temper so hot that he began to mutter aloud:

"And what's a hundred and thirty-six million years to you, Madam? That Professor needn't blow. You were winking and blinking up there maybe a hundred and thirty-six million times before that date they are so proud of. The rocks can't tell any tales on you. You were doing your stunt up there long before there was anything down here but — God knows what! Let's leave that to the professors, Madam, you and me!"

This childish bitterness toward "millions" and professors was the result of several things. Two of

Before Breakfast

Grenfell's sons were "professors"; Harrison a distinguished physicist at thirty. This morning, however, Harrison had not popped up in his father's mind. Grenfell was still thinking of a pleasant and courtly scientist whom he had met on the boat yesterday — a delightful man who had, temporarily at least, wrecked Grenfell's life with civilities and information.

It was natural, indeed inevitable, that two clean, close-shaven gentlemen in tailored woods clothes, passengers on the worst tub owned by the Canadian Steamships Company and both bound for a little island off the Nova Scotia coast, should get into conversation. It was all the more natural since the scientist was accompanied by a lovely girl — his daughter.

It was a pleasure to look at her, just as it is a pleasure to look at any comely creature who shows breeding, delicate preferences. She had lovely eyes, lovely skin, lovely manners. She listened closely when Grenfell and her father talked, but she didn't bark up with her opinions. When he asked her about their life on the island last summer, he liked everything she said about the place and the people. She answered him lightly, as if her impressions could matter only to herself, but, having an opinion, it was only good manners to admit it. "Sweet, but decided," was his rough estimate.

Since they were both going to an island which wasn't even on the map, supposed to be known only to the motor launches that called after a catch of herring, it was natural that the two gentlemen should talk about that bit of wooded rock in the sea. Grenfell always liked to talk about it to the right person. At first he thought Professor Fairweather was a right person. He had felt alarm when Fairweather mentioned that last summer he had put up a portable house on the shore about two miles from Grenfell's cabin. But he added that it would soon vanish as quietly as it had come. His geological work would be over this autumn, and his portable house would be taken to pieces and shipped to an island in the South Pacific. Having thus reassured him, Fairweather carelessly, in quite the tone of weather-comment small talk, proceeded to wreck one of Grenfell's happiest illusions; the escape-avenue he kept in the back of his mind when he was at his desk at Grenfell & Saunders, Bonds. The Professor certainly meant no harm. He was a man of the world, urbane, not self-important. He merely remarked that the island was interesting geologically because the two ends of the island belonged to different periods, yet the ice seemed to have brought them both down together.

"And about how old would our end be, Professor?" Grenfell meant simply to express polite interest, but he gave himself away, parted with his only defence — indifference.

"We call it a hundred and thirty-six million years," was the answer he got.

"Really? That's getting it down pretty fine, isn't it? I'm just a blank where science is concerned. I went to work when I was thirteen — didn't have any education. Of course some business men read up on science. But I have to struggle with reports and figures a good deal. When I do read I like something human — the old fellows: Scott and Dickens and Fielding. I get a great kick out of them."

The Professor was a perfect gentleman, but he couldn't resist the appeal of ignorance. He had sensed in half an hour that this man loved the island. (His daughter had sensed it a year ago, as soon as she arrived there with her father. Something about his cabin, the little patch of lawn in front, and the hedge of wild roses that fenced it in, told her that.) In their talk Professor Fairweather had come to realize that this man had quite an unusual feeling for the island, therefore he would certainly like to know more about it — all he could tell him!

The sun leaped out of the sea — the planet vanished. Grenfell rejected his eye-drops. Why patch up? What was the use . . . of anything? Why tear a man loose from his little rock and shoot him out into the eternities? All that stuff was inhuman. A man had his little hour, with heat and cold and a time-sense suited to his endurance. If

you took that away from him you left him spine-
less, accidental, unrelated to anything. He himself was, he realized, sitting in his bathrobe by his
washstand, limp! No wonder: what a night!
What a dreadful night! The speeds which ma-
chinists had worked up in the last fifty years were
mere baby-talk to what can go through a man's
head between dusk and daybreak. In the last ten
hours poor Grenfell had travelled over seas and
continents, gone through boyhood and youth,
founded a business, made a great deal of money,
and brought up an expensive family. (There were
three sons, to whom he had given every advantage and who had turned out well, two of them
brilliantly.) And all this meant nothing to him
except negatively — "to avoid worse rape," he
quoted Milton to himself.

Last night had been one of those nights of rev-
elation, revaluation, when everything seems to
come clear . . . only to fade out again in the
morning. In a low cabin on a high red cliff over-
hanging the sea, everything that was shut up in

him, under lock and bolt and pressure, simply broke jail, spread out into the spaciousness of the night, undraped, unashamed.

When his father died, Henry had got a job as messenger boy with the Western Union. He always remembered those years with a certain pride. His mother took in sewing. There were two little girls, younger than he. When he looked back on that time, there was nothing in it to be ashamed of. Those are the years, he often told the reformers, that make character, make proficiency. A business man should have early training, like a pianist, *at the instrument*. The sense of responsibility makes a little boy a citizen: for him there is no "dangerous age." From his first winter with the telegraph company he knew he could get on if he tried hard, since most lads emphatically did not try hard. He read law at night, and when he was twenty was confidential clerk with one of the most conservative legal firms in Colorado.

Everything went well until he took his first long vacation — bicycling in the mountains above Colorado Springs. One morning he was pedalling hard uphill when another bicycle came round a curve and collided with him; a girl coasting. Both riders were thrown. She got her foot caught in her wheel; sprain and lacerations. Henry ran two miles down to her hotel and her family. New York people; the father's name was a legend in Henry's credulous Western world. And they liked him, Henry, these cultivated, clever, experienced people! The mother was the ruling power — remarkable woman. What she planned, she put through — relentless determination. He ought to know, for he married that only daughter one year after she coasted into him. A warning unheeded, that first meeting. It was his own intoxicated vanity that sealed his fate. He had never been "made much over" before.

It had worked out as well as most marriages, he

supposed. Better than many. The intelligent girl had been no discredit to him, certainly. She had given him two remarkable sons, any man would be proud of them. . . .

Here Grenfell had flopped over in bed and suddenly sat up, muttering aloud. "But God, they're as cold as ice! I can't see through it. They've never lived at all, those two fellows. They've never run after the ball — they're so damned clever they don't *have* to. They just reach out and *take* the ball. Yes, fine hands, like their grandmother's; long . . . white . . . beautiful nails. The way Harrison picked up that book! I'm glad my paws are red and stubby."

For a moment he recalled sharply a little scene. Three days ago he was packing for his escape to this island. Harrison, the eldest son, the physicist, after knocking, had entered to his father's "Come in!" He came to ask who should take care of his personal mail (that which came to the house) if Miss O'Doyle should go on her vacation before he returned. He put the question rather grimly. The family seemed to resent the fact that, though he worked like a steam shovel while he was in town, when he went on a vacation he never told them how long he would be away or where he was going.

"Oh, I meant to tell you, Harrison, before I leave. But it was nice of you to think of it. Miss O'Doyle has decided to put off her vacation until the middle of October, and then she'll take a long one." He was sure he spoke amiably as he stood looking at his son. He was always proud of Harrison's fine presence, his poise and easy reserve. The little travelling bag (made to his order) which on a journey he always carried himself, never trusted to a porter, lay open on his writing table. On top of his pyjamas and razor case lay two little books bound in red leather. Harrison picked up one and glanced at the lettering on the back. *King Henry IV, Part I.*

"Light reading?" he remarked. Grenfell was stung by such impertinence. He resented any intrusion on his private, personal, non-family life.

"Light or heavy," he remarked dryly, "they're good company. And they're mighty human."

"They have that reputation," his son admitted. A spark flashed into Grenfell's eye. Was the fellow sarcastic, or merely patronizing?

"Reputation, hell!" he broke out. "I don't carry books around with my toothbrushes and razors on account of their reputation."

"No, I wouldn't accuse you of that." The young man spoke quietly, not warmly, but as if he meant it. He hesitated and left the room.

Sitting up in his bed in the small hours of the morning, Grenfell wondered if he hadn't flared up too soon. Maybe the fellow hadn't meant to be sarcastic. All the same he had no business to touch anything in his father's bag. That bag was like his coat pocket. Grenfell never bothered his family with his personal diversions, and he never intruded upon theirs. Harrison and his mother were a team — a close corporation! Grenfell respected it absolutely. No questions, no explanations demanded by him. The bills came in; Miss O'Doyle wrote the checks and he signed them.

He hadn't the curiosity, the vulgarity to look at them.

Of course, he admitted, there were times when he got back at the corporation just a little. That usually occurred when his dyspepsia had kept him on very light food all day and, the dinner at home happening to be "rich," he confined himself to graham crackers and milk. He remembered such a little dinner scene last month. Harrison and his mother came downstairs dressed to go out for the evening. Soon after the soup was served, Harrison wondered whether Koussevitzky would take the slow movement in the Brahms Second as he did last winter. His mother said she still remembered Muck's reading, and preferred it.

The theoretical head of the house spoke up. "I take it that this is Symphony night, and that my family are going. You have ordered the car? Well, I am going to hear John McCormack sing *Kathleen Mavourneen*."

His wife rescued him as she often did (in an

innocent, well-bred way) by refusing to recognize his rudeness. "Dear me! I haven't heard Mc-Cormack since he first came out in Italy years and years ago. His success was sensational. He was singing Mozart then."

Yes, when he was irritable and the domestic line-up got the better of him, Margaret, by being faultlessly polite, often saved the situation.

When he thought everything over, here in this great quiet, in this great darkness, he admitted that his shipwreck had not been on the family rock. The bitter truth was that his worst enemy was closer even than the wife of his bosom — was his bosom itself!

Grenfell had what he called a hair-trigger stomach. When he was in his New York office he worked like a whirlwind; and to do it he had to live on a diet that would have tried the leanest anchorite. The doctors said he did everything too hard. He knew that — he always had done things hard, from the day he first went to work for the

Western Union. Mother and two little sisters, no schooling — the only capital he had was the ginger to care hard and work hard. Apparently it was not the brain that desired and achieved. At least, the expense account came out of a very other part of one. Perhaps he was a throw-back to the Year One, when in the stomach was the only constant, never sleeping, never quite satisfied desire.

The humiliation of being "delicate" was worse than the actual hardship. He had found the one way in which he could make it up to himself, could feel like a whole man, not like a miserable dyspeptic. That way was by living rough, not by living soft. There wasn't a big-game country in North America where he hadn't hunted; mountain sheep in the wild Rockies, moose in darkest Canada, caribou in Newfoundland. Long before he could really afford it, he took four months out of every year to go shooting. His greatest triumph was a white bear in Labrador. His guide and packmen and canoe men never guessed that he was a frail man. Out there, up there, he wasn't! Out there he was just a "city man" who paid well; eccentric, but a fairly good shot. That was what he had got out of hard work and very good luck. He had got ahead wonderfully . . . but, somehow, ahead on the wrong road.

ॐ

At this point in his audit Grenfell had felt his knees getting cold, so he got out of bed, opened a clothes closet, and found his eiderdown bathrobe hanging on the hook where he had left it two summers ago. That was a satisfaction. (He liked to be orderly, and it made this cabin seem more his own to find things, year after year, just as he had left them.) Feeling comfortably warm, he ran up the dark window blinds which last night he had pulled down to shut out the disturbing sight of the stars. He bethought him of his eye-drops, tilted back his head, and there was that planet, serene, terrible and splendid, looking in at him . . . immortal beauty . . . yes, but only when somebody *saw* it, he fiercely answered back!

Before Breakfast

He thought about it until his head went round. He would get out of this room and get out quick. He began to dress — wool stockings, moccasins, flannel shirt, leather coat. He would get out and find his island. After all, it still existed. The Professor hadn't put it in his pocket, he guessed! He scrawled a line for William, his man Friday: "BREAKFAST WHEN I RETURN," and stuck it on a hook in his dining-car kitchen. William was "boarded out" in a fisherman's family. (Grenfell wouldn't stand anyone in the cabin with him. He wanted all this glorious loneliness for himself. He had paid dearly for it.)

He hurried out of the kitchen door and up the grassy hillside to the spruce wood. The spruces stood tall and still as ever in the morning air; the same dazzling spears of sunlight shot through their darkness. The path underneath had the dampness, the magical softness which his feet remembered. On either side of the trail yellow toadstools and white mushrooms lifted the heavy thatch of brown spruce needles and made little damp tents. Everything was still in the wood.

There was not a breath of wind; deep shadow and new-born light, yellow as gold, a little unsteady like other new-born things. It was blinking, too, as if its own reflection on the dewdrops was too bright. Or maybe the light had been asleep down under the sea and was just waking up.

"Hello, Grandfather!" Grenfell cried as he turned a curve in the path. The grandfather was a giant spruce tree that had been struck by lightning (must have been about a hundred years ago, the islanders said). It still lay on a slant along a steep hillside, its shallow roots in the air, all its great branches bleached greyish white, like an animal skeleton long exposed to the weather. Grenfell put out his hand to twitch off a twig as he passed, but it snapped back at him like a metal spring. He stopped in astonishment, his hand smarted, actually.

"Well, Grandfather! Lasting pretty well, I should say. Compliments! You get good drainage on this hillside, don't you?"

Ten minutes more on the winding uphill path

brought him to the edge of the spruce wood and out on a bald headland that topped a cliff two hundred feet above the sea. He sat down on a rock and grinned. Like Christian of old, he thought, he had left his burden at the bottom of the hill. Now why had he let Doctor Fairweather's perfectly unessential information give him a miserable night? He had always known this island existed long before he discovered it, and that it must once have been a naked rock. The soil-surface was very thin. Almost anywhere on the open downs you could cut with a spade through the dry turf and roll it back from the rock as you roll a rug back from the floor. One knew that the rock itself, since it rested on the bottom of the ocean, must be very ancient.

But that fact had nothing to do with the green surface where men lived and trees lived and blue flags and buttercups and daisies and meadow-sweet and steeplebush and goldenrod crowded one another in all the clearings. Grenfell shook himself and hurried along up the cliff trail. He crossed the first brook on stepping-stones. Must have been recent rain, for the water was rushing down the deep-cut channel with sound and fury till it leaped hundreds of feet over the face of the cliff and fell into the sea: a white waterfall that never rested.

The trail led on through a long jungle of black alder . . . then through a lazy, rooty, brown swamp . . . and then out on another breezy, grassy headland which jutted far out into the air in a horseshoe curve. There one could stand beside a bushy rowan tree and see four waterfalls, white as silver, pouring down the perpendicular cliff walls.

Nothing had changed. Everything was the same, and he, Henry Grenfell, was the same: the relationship was unchanged. Not even a tree blown down; the stunted beeches (precious because so few) were still holding out against a climate unkind to them. The old white birches that grew on the edge of the cliff had been so long beaten and tormented by east wind and north wind that they grew more down than up, and hugged the earth that was kinder than the

stormy air. Their growth was all one-sided, away
from the sea, and their land-side branches actually lay along the ground and crept up the hillside through the underbrush, persistent, nearly
naked, like great creeping vines, and at last, when
they got into the sunshine, burst into tender
leafage.

This knob of grassy headland with the bushy
rowan tree had been his vague objective when he
left the cabin. From this elbow he could look
back on the cliff wall, both north and south, and
see the four silver waterfalls in the morning light.
A splendid sight, Grenfell was thinking, and all
his own. Not even a gull — they had gone scream-
ing down the coast toward the herring weirs
when he first left his cabin. Not a living creature
— but wait a minute: there was something moving down there, on the shingle by the water's
edge. A human figure, in a long white bathrobe
— and a rubber cap! Then it must be a woman?
Queer. No island woman would go bathing at
this hour, not even in the warm inland ponds.
Yes, it was a woman! A girl, and he knew *what*

girl! In the miseries of the night he had forgotten her. The geologist's daughter.

How had she got down there without breaking her neck? She picked her way along the rough shingle; presently stopped and seemed to be meditating, seemed to be looking out at an old sliver of rock that was almost submerged at high tide. She opened her robe, a grey thing lined with white. Her bathing-suit was pink. If a clam stood upright and graciously opened its shell, it would look like that. After a moment she drew her shell together again — felt the chill of the morning air, probably. People are really themselves only when they believe they are absolutely alone and unobserved, he was thinking. With a quick motion she shed her robe, kicked off her sandals, and took to the water.

At the same moment Grenfell kicked off his moccasins. "Crazy kid! What does she think she's doing? This is the North Atlantic, girl, you can't treat it like that!" As he muttered, he was getting off his fox-lined jacket and loosening his braces. Just how he would get down to the shingle he didn't know, but he guessed he'd have to. He was getting ready while, so far, she was doing nicely. Nothing is more embarrassing than to rescue people who don't want to be rescued. The tide was out, slack — she evidently knew its schedule.

She reached the rock, put up her arms and rested for a moment, then began to weave her way back. The distance wasn't much, but Lord! the cold, — in the early morning! When he saw her come out dripping and get into her shell, he began to shuffle on his fur jacket and his moccasins. He kept on scolding. "Silly creature! Why couldn't she wait till afternoon, when the death-chill is off the water?"

He scolded her ghost all the way home, but he thought he knew just how she felt. Probably she used to take her swim at that hour last summer, and she had forgot how cold the water was. When she first opened her long coat the nip of the air had startled her a little. There was no one watching her, she didn't have to keep face — except to herself. That she had to do and no fuss about it. She hadn't dodged. She had gone out, and she had come back. She would have a happy day. He knew just how she felt. She surely did look like a little pink clam in her white shell!

He was walking fast down the winding trails. Everything since he left the cabin had been reassuring, delightful — everything was the same, and so was he! The air, or the smell of fir trees — something had sharpened his appetite. He was hungry. As he passed the grandfather tree he waved his hand, but didn't stop. Plucky youth is more bracing than enduring age. He crossed the sharp line from the deep shade to the sunny hillside behind his cabin and saw the wood smoke rising from the chimney. The door of the dining-car kitchen stood open, and the smell of coffee drowned the spruce smell and sea smell. William hadn't waited; he was wisely breakfasting.

As he came down the hill Grenfell was chuckling to himself: "Anyhow, when that first amphibious frog-toad found his water-hole dried up behind him, and jumped out to hop along till he could find another — well, he started on a long hop."

PRINTER'S NOTE

This book is set in ELECTRA, *a Linotype face designed by* W. A. DWIGGINS. *This face cannot be classified as either "modern" or "old-style." It is not based on any historical model, nor does it echo any particular period or style. It avoids the extreme contrast between "thick" and "thin" elements that mark most "modern" faces, and attempts to give a feeling of fluidity, power, and speed.*

The book was composed, printed, and bound by THE PLIMPTON PRESS, *Norwood, Massachusetts. The typography and binding are based on designs by* W. A. DWIGGINS.